TROUBLED

VOLUME 1: BREWING TROUBLE

SPACE

A K DUBOFF

Published by BDL Press

ISBN: 1658831802
ISBN-13: 978-1658831802

0 9 8 7 6 5 4 3 2 1

Produced in the United States of America

TABLE OF CONTENTS

CHAPTER 1

SHOT IN THE FOOT

— — —

SHOOTING himself in the foot with another business-deal-gone-wrong took on new meaning for Jack Tressler as he stared down the barrel of a real gun pointed toward his actual foot.

"Really, this is all a terrible misunderstanding," Jack tried to explain.

"Misunderstanding or not, you're a dead man." Svetlana Korinov charged her laser pistol while a handful of women in her crew looked on with amusement around him in the freighter's cargo bay. Her reputation for being the most powerful weapons smuggler in the sector showed in her pistol choice—sleek, shiny, and with pink accents on the barrel that made it clear she would be judged by no one. "I'll incinerate you piece by piece, and I'll enjoy every second."

Jack held up his hands and plastered on the most charming smile his mediocre looks allowed. "While I'm sure killing me would bring you great short-term satisfaction—I mean, who *doesn't* like to start out Monday morning with a revenge killing—what else would it really accomplish? Wouldn't you rather find out who stole your ship in the first place?"

Svetlana's violet eyes narrowed to slits beneath her exaggerated eyeliner. "Yes, but how could you possibly be of any use to me?"

"Me? Useful?" Jack forced a smug chuckle and smoothed back his blond hair with one hand. "Do you have any idea who I am?"

The weapons dealer activated Jack's holopin she was holding in her free hand, displaying his credentials. "Jack Tressler, age thirty-four. Outstanding warrants on five planets and banned from a sixth for... inappropriate yodeling?" She raised a quizzical eyebrow.

"Hey, it was *very* appropriate at the time. The authorities and I just didn't see eye-to-eye."

"Of course. And what about the forty-eight thousand credits in unpaid debts?"

Jack made a dismissive flip of his wrist. "Petty cash. That'll all be settled up after my next job."

"The one you intended to complete with my ship?" Svetlana asked.

"Well, yeah..." Granted, Jack hadn't known that it was stolen at the time when he'd purchased it from the third-party seller. In retrospect, he should have realized the terms of sale were too good to be true. Misfortune often came his way, especially when he tried to accomplish anything through proper channels. The fact that he had legitimately purchased the ship with the intention to use it for smuggling was beside the point; the ship's title was supposed to be free and clear. Unfortunately, it was looking like this misstep may be his last.

Svetlana scoffed. "You're a small-time criminal incapable of following through with his promises. I'd be doing everyone a favor if I end you." She altered the handgun's aim from Jack's foot to his head.

"Whoa, whoa!" Jack raised his hands again with renewed urgency. "You stopped reading too soon. You didn't get to the part about me being a legendary detective."

"You mean your one-time role as Sherlock in a primary school play?"

Jack lowered his hands. "Wow, you really *did* read my file."

"Your acting career won't help uncover who stole my ship, which confirms that you're utterly useless to me."

"Did you watch a recording of the play? You have to admit that an eight-year-old detective is adorable."

"Enough!" Svetlana took a step forward.

"Actually," a woman in her late-twenties standing in the throng behind Svetlana cut in, "we could use someone to modify for our next venture."

Svetlana lowered her weapon partway, which Jack hardly found to be an improvement since that meant it was pointing directly at his groin. Nonetheless, 'modify' sounded like a status upgrade from 'dead'.

"If I can be of service..." Jack began tentatively.

"I don't know if he's worth the trouble, Alyssa," Svetlana stated.

Alyssa looked Jack over, her tawny eyes partially obscured by dark, side-swept bangs. "I can handle him."

Svetlana sighed and deactivated her laser pistol. "Fine. If he assists and is successful, his debt to me will be forgiven."

Jack perked up. "You won't regret this!"

"I already do," Svetlana muttered as she holstered her handgun. "Prep him for surgery." She headed for the cargo bay door leading to the rest of the freighter.

Two women hung back with Alyssa, and the other dozen followed Svetlana toward the exit.

"Oh, right... the 'modifications'," Jack gulped. "What exactly—"

"We need to replace your eye," Alyssa stated with the matter-of-factness of a tax auditor.

"My eye?"

She nodded. "Your left eye. You will be fitted with a multispectral camera that will feed directly into your brain."

"That sounds..."

"It's minor brain surgery, don't worry," Alyssa said. "Morine has done it at least once before."

Jack crossed his arms. "Yeah, about that..."

"It's the implant or an execution. Take your pick."

"No Option C?"

Alyssa groaned and turned back toward her boss. "Svetl—!"

"Wait, I'll do it!" Jack interrupted.

"Great. You'll hardly notice a difference."

—

Jack's eye fluttered open.

A bright light shone down on him, obscuring his view of the room at first. Then, a figure next to his bed came into focus.

"That is... horrifying." Alyssa's nose wrinkled.

"What?"

Alyssa took a step backward from his medical bed. "Well, the apparatus didn't quite fit."

"What do you mean?" As Jack asked the question, he realized that the left half of his vision was missing. He reached toward his face and felt a metal protrusion coming from where his left eye used to be. "Great."

"I'm sure it'll seem natural in no time."

"Liar."

Alyssa shrugged. "I tried."

Jack sighed and sat up on the medical bed. His head

swam. "I didn't realize this was going to half-blind me."

"The implant isn't activated yet—this was just the installation. We'll give you another day or two to heal before we turn it on."

"When are you going to tell me what it's for?"

The woman eyed him. "Someone's cranky."

"Well, how do you expect me to be?" Jack shot back. "I bought a ship that I didn't know was stolen, you held me at gunpoint, and now you've taken my eye—my *favorite* eye, I might add. Aside from my terrible luck, I don't know why this is happening or what your aim is."

Alyssa stuck out her lower lip in a mock display of pity. "It has been a rough few days for you, hasn't it?"

Jack ignored her and slid off the bed. His sense of equilibrium was almost nonexistent, and he needed to keep both his hands on the mattress to prevent himself from toppling over.

He'd be the first to admit that there were a number of questionable decisions in his past. Between dropping out of school, petty crimes, and a handful of more serious infractions, he hadn't set himself up for a promising future. But, when it came to taking care of his grandmother—the only person who'd ever seemed to believe in him—he'd go to any lengths to make sure her living expenses were covered. Getting conscripted into a pirate gang, however, was a new low.

"Let's get this over with," he said, taking an awkward step forward like a newborn foal.

Alyssa rushed over and placed her arm around his waist. "Okay, you want to know what's going on? I'll show you."

She led him out of the exam room—more accurately, a storage closet with a second-hand hospital bed and tarp on the floor—into a drab hallway. Jack took in the details of the corridor and strained to identify any background mechanical sounds that might provide more information about his location. Having grown up on all manner of spacecraft, picking up such tones was second-nature. As near as he could tell, they were no longer on Svetlana's freighter where he'd been interrogated, but rather somewhere in the depths of a space station.

They traversed the dimly lit hall lined with utility conduits and eventually arrived at a hatch. Alyssa spun the manual wheel to unseal the door, then leaned her shoulder against it. The hatch creaked open.

The other side was far more welcoming than where Jack had awoken after the surgery—an open room furnished with two white couches, an assortment of potted plants, and various other fixtures that enhanced the appearance of a comfortable living room. Most surfaces were white and shiny to a degree that Jack considered completely impractical; even without the worry of tracking mud in from outside, the fingerprint smudges could way too easily get out of control.

"Where are we?" he asked.

Alyssa re-sealed the hatch using a lever that folded back into a disguised recess within the wall. "This is *Luxuria*, our main base. If I told you any more, Svetlana would probably have me kill you."

"Keeping it vague works for me," Jack hastily replied.

"But, now that you're sporting that neat little piece of hardware, I can share exactly what it is you're going to do for us." She stepped over to a low table between the two couches and activated a translucent touch-surface panel inset in the top. She navigated through a menu and made a selection. The tabletop flickered as a hologram of a slowly rotating cylindrical object appeared above it.

Jack studied the image. "I haven't a clue what that is."

"It's a micro energy core, or MEC," Alyssa explained. "It's a new prototype that was developed by GiganCorp Labs."

"They're the giant, corporate research company, right?"

"The very one." Alyssa scowled with disdain. "MECs were completely theoretical until this prototype was developed. The potential applications are endless—biomedical, backup power, kitchen appliances..."

"And let me guess: weapons," Jack completed.

"Correct."

Jack shook his head and groaned. "Svetlana wants said prototype, huh?"

Alyssa nodded. "And you're going to help me steal it."

CHAPTER 2

A TERRIBLE PLAN

— — —

JACK gingerly itched around his cybernetic eye. "Break into GiganCorp Labs and steal their prototype?"

"That's right," Alyssa acknowledged without batting an eye.

"You said that with a straight face."

"Because I'm completely serious."

"But that's insane!" Jack exclaimed. "Their security—"

"Won't be that big of a deal," Alyssa cut in. "At least not with the aid of that fancy Thingamado in your head."

Jack crossed his arms. "This is all a joke to you, isn't it?"

Alyssa rolled her eyes. "You're just going to have to trust me."

"Says the woman who cut out my eye!"

"I'll admit that wasn't the best way to start out this relationship. But keep in mind that I did save your life."

Jack scoffed. "Yeah, spared me so I could instead rot

on a prison planet after we're caught trying to steal a gizmo from what I can only imagine is a highly secure research facility. That was really considerate."

"MEC," Alyssa corrected.

"Oh, so you get to use 'thingamado' and I'm not allowed to use 'gizmo'?"

"Thingamado is literally the brand name. Clearly you didn't hear the capital 't'."

Jack didn't have a good response to that. "Oh."

"Anyway," Alyssa continued, "we won't get caught."

"How can you be so sure?"

"Because I'm awesome." She closed the hologram on the tabletop and the screen returned to its clear, glass-like state.

"So I'm not doing this alone?" Jack clarified.

"Oh no," Alyssa laughed. "No, you'd most certainly be killed. Like, immediately."

"I thought security wouldn't be a problem with my cool eye-thing?"

She shook her head. "That's only a small part of it. I mean, honestly, you're just a tool for me to use so I didn't have to do that to myself."

The words cut deep. "Ouch."

Momentary regret flashed across Alyssa's face. "Sorry. I probably shouldn't have said that out loud."

"You think?" Jack sat down on one of the white couches, massaging his temples. "I do appreciate you stopping my execution and all, but I wasn't trying to wrong any of you. One bad purchasing decision and my life has sort of been derailed in the last twenty-four hours."

"You were actually unconscious for three days but..." Alyssa shook her head. "That's irrelevant. Look, we're going to have to work together, so let's just start over and get the job done."

"I guess I don't really have much of a choice, do I?"

"Not really, no. Unless you want Svetlana to shoot you."

"Still not liking that option."

Alyssa cracked a smile. "All right. In that case, I should probably show you to your quarters so you can get some real sleep—that anesthesia doesn't make for quality rest, even if it has been three days."

"I was going to say, I feel like I should be way better rested."

"Well, you better be after tonight because we have quite the journey ahead of us."

"This isn't just a simple theft?" Jack questioned.

"Hopefully everything will be straightforward once we get there, but we'll need to stock up on some supplies first, and some of those items won't be easy to obtain."

"Such as...?"

Alyssa winced. "A nano induction module."

"You *have* to be kidding."

"I know, I know. I have a plan."

Jack raised his one good eyebrow. "There isn't any reasonable approach for dealing with the Winkelson Brothers."

"You know they hate that name." Alyssa smirked.

"Sorry, but I could never quite get on board with 'Lords of Doom'."

"Right? They haven't done one remotely menacing thing."

Jack flourished his hands. "Precisely. Frankly, I've just always avoided them because of the legendary stench."

"Which is not insurmountable," Alyssa pointed out. "That's why the first step of my plan is to catch them on a shower day."

"That's what, once a month?"

"Not if we *make* it a shower day," she grinned.

"And how is that accomplished?"

"Soup."

Jack's eye widened. Clearly she'd lost her mind. "Come again?"

"Well, chili, technically. There's this particular brand—they buy it in barrels. Apparently the shelf life is phenomenal."

"The stench is suddenly making a whole lot more sense."

"I know! So, I'm thinking there's going to be a little mishap with the delivery."

"What kind of mishap?" Jack asked cautiously.

"Perhaps a simulated eruption of an air bubble trapped during the packaging process, which would just happen to correspond to when the barrel is opened for a quality control check."

Jack smiled. "You're quite devious."

"It's a gift. Needless to say, soup everywhere and showers would be in order."

"That's assuming they have any sense of decency—which is fairly well established that they don't," Jack countered.

"I forgot to mention the defective feather pillows that will 'accidentally' be added to their order."

"*Now* we're talking."

Alyssa grinned. "So, while they're busy trying to remove soupy feathers without permanently destroying their plumbing system, we should be able to sneak in, crack their vault, and take a nano induction module."

"Or *all* of them, if we're going to that trouble."

"Good point."

"But," Jack raised his finger, "the safe-cracking bit..."

"Yeah, that's going to be tricky. That's why we'll need Finn."

"And where is Finn?"

"In prison."

Jack sighed and shook his head. "*Which* prison?"

Alyssa inched back on the couch adjacent to Jack. "Hellana," she said under her breath.

"Oh, come on..."

"Look, it's only hard to break out of. It's plenty easy to get in."

Jack groaned. "But to get someone out you need to *break out!*"

"It shouldn't be a problem for Triss."

"And let me guess, Triss is—"

"Watching a vid next door," Alyssa interrupted. "She's going ahead to get things prepped in the morning."

"Oh."

Alyssa smiled. "So, all we have to do is break Finn out of prison, steal the nano induction module from the Winkelson Brothers, and then gather a little bit of radioactive material from Thandor VII so we can break into the GiganCorp research lab. Easy."

Jack frowned. "You didn't mention the radioactive part before."

"I didn't? Probably because it's barely worth mentioning." She shrugged.

"Alyssa, this is a terrible plan."

CHAPTER 3

POPULAR WITH THE LADIES

— — —

A proper night's rest left Jack feeling much improved, but he couldn't help reflecting on the disastrous turn of events. While things hadn't been going great lately—or ever—he had at least maintained some sense of autonomy with his former dealings. Becoming a half-blind captive to a possibly crazed weapons dealer wasn't part of his life plan.

He decided the misfortune could be traced back to one fateful night on Raylen II, which had involved copious tequila bombs and anchovy-based finger foods. Granted, he couldn't actually remember the night, but the gap in his memory seemed like a reasonable place to pinpoint for his decidedly downward trajectory as late.

The sleeping chamber where he'd been deposited for the night was actually an empty closet with a blanket on the floor. He was thankful for the blanket and slightly less thankful that the floor was inexplicably sloped at fifteen degrees and he kept sliding into the wall while he slept.

Nonetheless, he awoke feeling happy to still be alive,

despite his itchy eye implant, and was ready to tackle Alyssa's crazy plan.

He was roused from his blanket cocoon by a knock on the door. Without waiting for him to reply, the door swung inward and Alyssa peered in.

"Ready?" she asked.

"After that talk about the Winkelson Brothers, I don't suppose I could get a shower myself?" Jack asked.

Alyssa nodded. "I was going to request it. This way."

She led him down the hall through the living room area to a sliding door. "Wait here a minute," she instructed and stepped inside.

Thirty seconds later, a different woman emerged from the room wearing only a towel. She gave Jack a look of distaste as she passed by.

Alyssa exited right behind her. "It's all yours," she told him. "We don't exactly get many male visitors around here."

"Not even for fun?" he asked.

"Ew. Why would we do that when we have each other?" She stepped aside. "Go clean up. I'll be waiting out here."

Jack took a quick shower and ran his clothes through the ultrasonic cleaner. By the time he was re-dressed in his gray shirt, black flight jacket, and charcoal pants he was feeling more like himself, despite the missing eye. He took several minutes to inspect the surgical site and replacement apparatus.

True to Alyssa's initial assessment, the modification was a touch on the horrifying side. The metal eye protruded from his eye socket, revealing glowing blue lights. An artificial iris at the center was presently closed. The skin around the artificial eye was red and tender, but it appeared that the wound was healing. Knowing there wasn't much he could do about the disfiguration at this juncture, he decided to invent an epic war story to tell the ladies about how he lost the eye—like saving an entire village from a meteor shower that happened to correspond with an attack from extradimensional aliens. Yeah, he was a hero.

Smiling to himself as he thought about his fictional escapades, he left the bathroom and found Alyssa waiting on the couch in the common room for him.

"Took you long enough," she muttered, rising to her feet. She stepped over toward the corridor leading through the far wall. "We're behind schedule."

"For the jailbreak?" Jack asked, jogging to catch up with her brisk pace.

"More or less. Triss is waiting for us."

Jack beamed. "Look at you using 'us'! It's almost like we're a team."

"Don't get any ideas," Alyssa cautioned. "I'm authorized to use deadly force if you so much as look at me funny."

"No need to get all defensive."

"I'm not—" Alyssa cut herself off and groaned. "I should have gotten you a muzzle to go with that freak eye."

"What happened to 'us'?" Jack attempted to bat his eyelashes—normally a surefire move for melting hearts—but the singular eye made the move decidedly more difficult.

Alyssa ignored him and walked faster.

She led him down the corridor to a lift, which deposited them in another hallway. At the end of that, a large sliding door was marked 'Shuttle Bay'.

"We're taking a ship?" Jack questioned.

"Obviously. I think you're familiar with it."

He perked up. "The *Lucille*?"

"That was *your* name for it," Alyssa replied. "Svetlana has always known it as the *Little Princess*."

"That name was never going to work with my image."

"Congratulations. Consider your image revised."

The *Little Princess* was somewhat larger than its name suggested—stretching fifty meters long and twenty meters tall. It was a mass production model with a generic central body, wide wing base, and three thrusters in the rear. He'd seen countless others like it in his travels. It was one of those ships that a traveler would come across in any corner of the galaxy while going on some crazy adventure or another.

"You have exceptionally boring taste in starships, you know," Alyssa commented as they walked across the nearly empty hangar toward the vessel. "Of all the ships to steal, you had to pick one of these."

"Again, I *bought it*," Jack retorted. "Blame the thief for their bad taste. I just wanted something modest and affordable to get my business going."

"Were you seriously trying to do something respectable?"

"Well, my grandmother's housing costs keep going up, and I thought maybe if I could get my own venture going I'd be able to take care of her better."

"Oh." A smile lit up Alyssa's eyes. "That's actually really sweet."

Jack shrugged. "She was there for me when I was growing up, even when my parents weren't. All I've wanted is to give back to her, but then some new setback like this will happen." He swept his hand to encompass the room and sighed. "Anyway, smuggling is pretty difficult with forged credentials, so I bought the ship. I needed the paperwork to look good in case I was ever questioned."

"You can fit maybe four people and a crate of food in one of these. That's terrible for smuggling."

"Lemme guess, you haven't been out to Corican, have you?" Jack asked.

"No, why?"

"Well, the engines are bulky on these guys. But, if

you're okay with slower acceleration, you can swap out one of the turbo tanks for an extra cargo hold—something that no inspector is looking for."

Alyssa's eyes widened momentarily. "That is rather clever."

"I never got the chance to make the alteration, but it's something Svetlana might be interested in."

"All right, I guess maybe you aren't as clueless as we thought."

Jack smiled. "See? Live and learn."

She smiled back. "Let's see what kind of score we can get to help your grandma."

They made the final approach to the vessel, and Alyssa used a control panel under a hatch on the side of the ship to input an access code for the passenger door. It chirped with acceptance and the door folded down from the side wall to form a ramp.

"I think all of your things are still in here," she said as they entered. "Based on the smell of feet, I'm guessing that includes your laundry."

"It's not equipped with an ultrasonic cleaner—which is surprising given Svetlana's apparent fastidiousness."

Alyssa eyed him with a hint of surprise. "That was a big word for you."

"That's not the only big—"

"I'm going to stop you right there. No."

Jack sighed. "Too good of an opening. I had to try."

She nodded. "Props for that."

Everything did appear to be in order based on how Jack had left it. He passed through the narrow hallway that ran the length of the vessel on the starboard side and entered into the compact living area amidships, which consisted of a couch, and couple of chairs, and a galley complete with a small dining table. He scanned over the contents of a cabinet on the back wall, secured by a plexiglass door.

"It is still here!" Jack slid the door open and pulled out a slim, elongated metal case. It opened on a hinge along the long edge, and he extracted a piece of straw from the cradle inside the case.

"Is that hay?" Alyssa asked with one eyebrow raised.

"Only if you want to be all backworlds about it," Jack replied as he placed the stalk between his teeth. "This is artisan straw."

Alyssa's expression of profound distaste didn't diminish. "And why is it in your mouth?"

"It's sophisticated and gives me character."

"Um, no."

Jack scoffed. "You're just envious because you don't have your own."

Alyssa let out a long breath between her teeth. "Did someone really tell you that holding a piece of straw in your mouth would make you look cool?"

"She didn't tell me—she *enlightened* me."

"She was messing with you."

Jack shrugged off the statement.

"No, seriously," Alyssa insisted. "Pretty sure this is how it went down: you failed hard while attempting to flirt with her, she had some quick wit and the kind of charm you can't train, and she devised a delightful gag that she still jokes about with her friends to this day."

"You don't know what you're talking about."

Alyssa grinned. "Oh, but I do. I see the doubt in your eye."

Jack faltered. "No, I mean... Maybe it was kind of strange how she smirked while she suggested it."

"Had you made any sort of lewd comment?"

"That depends on your definition of 'lewd'..."

Alyssa nodded with satisfaction, snickering. "Yep, that's what happened. She wanted to make you look like you had an oral fixation."

"A what? No." Jack shook his head.

"Yeah, and I don't mean in the kind of way ladies would find alluring."

"Sucking on a piece of straw isn't—"

Alyssa could barely contain her giggling. "Lemme guess, she suggested that you find the longest, thickest piece of straw you can and slowly—"

"Stop. Stop! Please." Jack spat out the straw and stomped on it.

She paused her cackling for two seconds and then burst into another giggle fit. "This is too good."

"No more straw. Happy?"

Eyes tearing, Alyssa regained her composure. "You know, I actually kind of liked it."

Jack was trying to think of a witty retort when an alarm sounded in the hangar.

CHAPTER 4

THE MISADVENTURE BEGINS

— — —

"THAT'S not good," Alyssa said with a frown.

"What is that sound and why is it so alarming?" Jack asked, holding his hands over his ears.

"The *Luxuria* has been breached."

"What?" Jack shouted.

Alyssa removed his hands from over his ears. "The spaceport is compromised. We need to go—now!"

Jack's pulse spiked. "What happened?"

"I have no idea, but that alarm means a decompression is imminent." Alyssa's previously unflappable demeanor was frayed around the edges. "Seal the door. I'll get the engines warmed up."

Jack nodded and returned to the hatch where they'd entered. He used the control panel to raise the door ramp and then manually locked it down with a lever. The alarm in the hangar was nearly silent with the door closed, though it still reverberated along the hull.

By the time he was finished, he could feel the vibration from the engines under foot. He ran the short length to the cockpit at the front of the craft. Two seats faced a three-panel window and an instrument panel with a combination of button control and touch interfaces. A HUD on the central window was presently displaying the engine initialization progress.

"Have you tried asking the station what the alarm is about?" Jack asked Alyssa as he took the seat on the right.

"No response," she replied, keeping her gaze focused on the systems checks displayed on the HUD. "We'll meet Triss at our planned rendezvous."

"I'm in support of any plan that involves being somewhere other than here."

Alyssa scowled at the controls. "And we *would* be somewhere else already if this ship didn't take an eternity to warm up."

"That's on your boss, not me," Jack said, raising his hands in defense. "I would have gone for something other than the base model if I'd had a halfway decent budget."

"She would have, but—"

The ship lurched to the side.

"Uh…" Jack began.

Alyssa rose partway from her seat to get a better view out the front window. She immediately sat back down and strapped into the flight harness.

Jack only needed a moment's glance outside to do the same thing. There was a hole in the hangar wall, and it wasn't an open door.

He had barely strapped in when the *Little Princess* careened across the floor toward the vacuum.

Alyssa made rapid entries on the control panel to force a quick-start of the engines—a risky maneuver indoors, but launching on an uncontrolled vector into a potential debris field was way more dangerous.

"Argh!" she exclaimed with frustration when the systems were nonresponsive.

"You have to reverse the polarity!" Jack shouted.

"That doesn't even make sense!"

"It works... for some reason. Just do it!" he insisted.

Alyssa made the necessary inputs to modify the power flow through the engines. System lights lit up green across the board.

"Huh," she murmured, dumbstruck.

"Fly!" Jack shouted, involuntarily ducking as the ship passed dangerously close to a cargo crane that had been wrenched free from inside the hangar.

The *Little Princess* and loose equipment from the hangar passed through the maw in the side of the station and entered into open space.

Alyssa grabbed the controls and fired the thrusters to begin countering their uncontrolled spin away from the station. With careful maneuvering, the tumbling slowed and she was able to swing the ship around under her control to get a view of the *Luxuria*.

Rather, what was left of the *Luxuria*.

"Stars..." Alyssa breathed.

Jack gasped as he took in the sight. The hole in the hangar was one of several gashes around the structure. It appeared that the station had resembled a four-pronged star in its whole state, but one of the arms was broken off entirely, and it appeared that all power had been lost.

"I guess that explains why they weren't replying to your calls," Jack murmured.

"Did any of them make it out?" Tears were forming in Alyssa's eyes as she took in the destruction, searching for signs of escape pods. "What could have done this?"

Her question was immediately answered by a near-miss laser blast across the nose of the vessel.

Jack spotted the origin of the shot off their port side—a nasty-looking warship with unnecessary spikes along the dorsal support beam, armored plating, and comically large guns. Many, many guns.

He gulped. "I'm going to suggest we jump to—"

The stars were a blur outside his window before he could complete the sentence.

The hyperspace jump had Jack pinned against the back of his seat for the initial five seconds of acceleration. As the ship achieved velocity, he was able to breathe normally again, and he took several deep breaths to calm his racing heart.

"Do you have any idea what's going on?" he stammered.

Alyssa set the autopilot and slouched in her seat. "I'd heard rumors, but didn't think they'd come after us."

"Who?"

"The Vorlox."

Jack shook his head. "Can't say I've heard of them."

"Consider yourself lucky." Alyssa ran her hands down the side of her face. "Do you think anyone made it out in time?"

"I have no idea." It was then that Jack remembered the women on the station were—or had been—her friends. That was a lot of potential loss to process. "I'm sure they're fine," he added.

"We'll find out when we meet up with Triss, I suppose," Alyssa said. "Just need to stay focused on the mission."

"You're being rather calm about this, considering that your home was just destroyed."

"I wouldn't say it was my home, exactly. And they were my friends, but not really a family."

Jack examined her out of the corner of his eye. "You seemed ready to take some pretty big risks for them."

"Not for them," Alyssa clarified. "This was a job for me."

"But still..."

"We all just try to find our way through life."

"Wow, that got deep suddenly."

Alyssa shrugged it off. "It's been a tough few minutes. Can you not make a joke for once?"

"Sorry, it's involuntary."

"Yeah, I got that impression." She sighed. "Look, if the Vorlox are after us, this may change the plan."

Jack was unnerved by the idea of having a crazed, heavily armored group of... "Wait, so who or what are the Vorlox, anyway? Aliens or—"

"Oh, no no," Alyssa cut in. "They're human, based on every account I've heard. They just spent a little too much time on spaceships with subpar radiation shielding. Rumors have been floating around about them attacking space stations and freighters."

"So, went kind of..." Jack circled his index finger horizontally near his ear.

"Yep. And murdery."

"That's unfortunate."

"Yeah..." She got a distant look in her eyes. "You're right, they probably got out."

Jack nodded. "That's the spirit! So, where are we meeting Triss?"

"A secret weapons dealer hangout," she replied. "Fortunately, Triss left an hour ago so I know she got out before the attack."

"That's a relief."

Alyssa's mouth twitched into a subtle smile. "Yeah, it is."

"Wait... you two are a thing, aren't you?" Jack realized.

"That doesn't matter," Alyssa shot back and turned her attention out the front window.

"Oh, come on—you can tell me!"

"Not important right now," she said. Her tone had turned serious.

Then, Jack noticed the warning light flashing on the control console. "What's wrong?"

"The fuel line must have been damaged in the attack. We're running on fumes."

"Where are we?"

Alyssa grabbed the yoke on the flight controls. "We're about to find out."

CHAPTER 5

A STROKE OF LUCK

— — —

THE *Little Princess* dropped out of hyperspace within half a kilometer of an asteroid.

"Whoa!" Alyssa quickly buried the yoke to the left, away from the giant rock.

"That could have been better or a whole lot worse," Jack commented as soon as they were clear.

"Dropping directly into an asteroid would be bad, but drifting endlessly through space without any fuel might be worse."

"Well, we're in luck." Jack pointed up ahead.

Alyssa's gaze followed his arm. Their new course was leading directly toward a space station built around another asteroid. "Well, that's convenient."

"I'll take it."

The space station was a rambling sort often found in the more backwater systems, cobbled together with random parts salvaged from other vessels. Though not pretty to look at, it should at least have a fueling depot to help get them back on track.

Alyssa directed the *Little Princess* to the tanker at the far end of the station—the most likely location to procure fuel.

A chirp sounded on the front console.

"Docking control," Jack said and accepted the communication request on the holodisplay in front of him.

"Business and duration?" a woman asked in the monotone of someone who needed to ask the same question dozens of time each day.

"Fueling and... however long fueling takes," Jack replied.

"Go to Berth E-792," the dock controller replied and ended the call.

"You really have no idea how to be a functional adult, do you?" Alyssa questioned.

Jack groaned. "What did I do wrong now?"

"Any worthwhile pilot knows exactly how long it takes to fuel their vessel."

"Guess what? I owned this ship for eight hours before Svetlana's goons came after me, so it's not like I really had time to read the instruction manual."

"Excuses!"

Jack then noticed the smirk playing on Alyssa's lips. "You're just messing with me."

She gave him a sidelong glance. "Well yeah. You make it entirely too easy."

"I really can't figure out your angle. You save my life—sort of—then make everything worse, then are mean to me, then joke. I don't know what to think."

She was silent for several moments. "This whole thing wasn't my idea," she replied at last. "I don't have a personal problem with you—actually, I find you kind of entertaining in that way you'd watch a slow motion video of someone's fail."

"Hey!"

"Sorry." She blushed slightly. "But in all seriousness, there are no ill feelings on my end. This was a chance for me to use Svetlana's motivations for my own benefit."

"What are *you* after?"

"Now is not the time or place to get into that." Alyssa kept her gaze focused ahead as she maneuvered the ship toward the designated berth highlighted on the HUD.

"Not even a hint?"

"Let's just say that both of our problems will go away if we can pull this off. And it will require us to work as a team. A win-win."

Jack examined her in the pilot's chair. "Okay... What do I have to do?"

"Follow my lead, don't question what I tell you to do, even if it seems crazy, and trust that your money problems will soon be a thing of the past."

"Sounds like wishful thinking."

She shrugged. "You might be surprised."

They pulled into Berth E-792 and docking clamps secured the *Little Princess* to the station. Alyssa coordinated fueling with the docking attendant while Jack took inventory of their supplies. He'd been in the process of figuring out his provisions when he'd been stunned and dragged back to Svetlana's base. Though only a matter of days prior, it felt like an eternity.

The incongruous sense of time passage was underscored by the odd rapport he'd developed with Alyssa. He'd begun the day in the role of prisoner, but over the past hour it seemed like she was viewing him more as a business partner in whatever her master plan may be. Though strange and unexpected, he wasn't opposed. Given his chronic ill-fated ventures, he was eager to jump on any opportunity to try something new. Losing an eye was less than ideal, but in the larger scheme of things that was a small price to pay for the possibility of getting out of debt and on the path to success.

"Should be all fueled up in twenty minutes," Alyssa announced, coming to find Jack in the store room behind a hatch in the living area.

"We have rations for two weeks. Will that be enough?" he asked her.

"That should work," she confirmed. "We can always stock up after we get Finn out of Hellana."

"Oh, right. I forgot about that part of the plan."

"It really won't be as difficult as you think," Alyssa insisted. "Triss is really good."

Jack made a dismissive shrug. "I guess I'll just do what I'm told."

She smiled. "So you *are* trainable. Excellent."

"Maybe you can make a functional adult out of me one of these days."

"Let's not go overboard," Alyssa said with a chuckle. "But speaking of functional, I should probably activate that implant."

"Oh right." Jack reached up to feel the eye. "What does it do, anyway?"

"Well, it will be able to detect things that we can't see with normal vision. Infrared, UV, and also electrical fields. In addition, it can generate signals in specific frequencies and patterns."

"Such as fooling a biometric scanner?" Jack asked.

"You've got it," she confirmed. "It's half of the key to breaking past GiganCorp's security."

"What's the other half?"

"Me, of course." She grinned.

"I have no doubt that your charm will win anyone over."

"That or my gunslinging. This really could go either way."

Jack chuckled. "All right. Well, I'm excited to have more than half my vision."

"It'll be better than before, once you get used to

cycling the modes." Alyssa directed Jack toward the couch. She pulled out a slim black case from her hip pocket and selected a delicate metal implement from inside. "Hold still," she instructed as she leaned over in front of him with the metal tool in hand.

He couldn't see what she was doing to his left eye, but he detected a slight pressure on the implant as she poked at it. Then, there was a flash of white light on the left side of his vision, followed by a 'Thingamado' logo with a progress bar loading in a circle around it. When the circle was completely full, his left field of vision restored in full color with only slight pixelation to differentiate the image from his organic eye.

"Oh that's *much* better!" he exclaimed. "Never again will I take depth perception for granted."

"It's on Normal mode right now, correct?"

"Seems that way."

Alyssa nodded and extended the metal implement toward his cybernetic eye—which was decidedly more unnerving now that he could see it coming toward him. She made contact and his vision switched to infrared. She appeared in a rainbow of color with bright red at her core and a mixture of green and yellow on her hands; in contrast, the ship in the background was mostly cool blue.

"This is really trippy," Jack murmured.

"But super handy for detecting guards in low light." Alyssa made another adjustment and his vision switched to UV.

The vibrant colors shifted to almost monochromatic, but he could suddenly make out details that were completely invisible to his other eye.

"What do you see?" Alyssa asked.

Jack looked around the room and his gaze rested on several stains on the couch. "Uh, looks like the UV is working just fine."

"All right, and now?" She made another adjustment.

His vision cycled to a spectacular display of the electromagnetic fields contained within the ship—everything from his own nerve impulses to the power conduits within the walls. Staring at Alyssa and being able to almost see her thinking weirded him out while simultaneously fascinating him. "Whoa," he managed to stammer.

"I've heard that one takes the longest to get used to."

"I'll say. But it's awesome!" Jack grinned. "I like collecting random, useful things."

"Good, because this one is a part of you now."

"I like to be prepared for anything—I'm used to things going wrong."

She made a final adjustment and his vision returned to normal. "Well, we're going to need this, for sure. In theory, you should be able to switch modes by thinking about it. That may take some practice to master."

"Nice."

Alyssa rose from her crouching position in front of him and smiled. "But for now, we have a jailbreak to plan."

CHAPTER 6

WHEN A PLAN COMES TOGETHER

— — —

AFTER getting the leak patched and paying for the fuel through an electronic credit transfer from Alyssa's account, the *Little Princess* was soon on its way to the rendezvous with Triss.

Alyssa had remained reticent about where the meetup would take place, but Jack was feeling comfortable enough with her that he was content to be along for the ride. Really, anyone willing to pick up the fuel bill was good in his book.

Two hours in hyperspace transit passed before the ship finally dropped back into normal space. Jack was surprised to see that their destination was absolutely in the middle of nowhere with nothing in sight. "Did you enter the right coordinates?" he asked.

She rolled her eyes. "What did I say about questioning me?" She manipulated the controls to rotate the ship one-hundred-eighty degrees. A ship four times the size of their own was in the space that had been right behind them. "Always drop out on the far side so you don't accidentally run into each other," she stated.

"Oh, right."

Alyssa directed the *Little Princess* to an airlock on the starboard side of the larger vessel and lined up their own hatch. With some careful maneuvering, she made the seal.

"Let's go." Alyssa rose from the pilot's chair and led them to the ship's main hatch. She double-checked the coupling and released the door seal.

The hatch on the other ship was already open and a red-headed woman was waiting in the doorway. She wilted with relief when she saw Alyssa and they ran to embrace one another.

"I didn't know if you'd made it out," the other woman murmured.

"Have you heard from anyone?" Alyssa asked, pulled out of the hug so she could look at her at arm's length.

"A few people, yes," the woman confirmed. "It sounds like everyone was able to get to escape pods, but many were captured by the Vorlox sometime after the attack."

Alyssa drew her in for a kiss and held her close. She pulled away after several seconds. "We move forward with the plan. We'll find a way to get them back once we have it."

"I know."

The other woman turned her attention to Jack standing awkwardly behind them. "Wow, that implant really didn't fit well."

"You must be Triss," Jack said.

"Yes," Alyssa replied. "Triss, Jack. Jack, Triss."

"Thanks for volunteering," Triss said to him.

"Didn't really have an option, but all in all it hasn't been that bad," he said. "Well, except for the eye. But this one seems pretty cool."

"Can we trust him?" Triss asked Alyssa.

Alyssa nodded. "He kind of grows on you. Just ignore

his innuendos."

"I can do that," her friend replied. "Everything's been prepped. Let's get ready to head down to Hellana."

"Oh, so we're actually going down into a maximum security prison," Jack muttered. "I thought maybe you had some sort of workaround where we could beam Finn out, or something."

"Well, we're not exactly going into the prison," Triss clarified. "And you don't have to do much for this part. Just watch and learn."

—

Even from space, Hellana was true to its name. The planet's surface was an inhospitable Hellscape of volcanic activity and massive blights. A lava field on the scale of an ocean marred the southern hemisphere, and only a tiny valley in a blackened region of the north looked to be remotely habitable.

"I think I'll stay here on the ship," Jack proclaimed as he looked out the main window on the bridge of the ship, the *Prancer*, which was functioning as their base.

"Nonsense! It'll be a good bonding exercise for us," Alyssa contended.

"In the way that skin bonds to rock when you melt to death?"

"No, of course not! It'll only be about sixty degrees Celsius. No melting at that temperature."

"It's a dry heat," Triss jumped in.

Alyssa flourished her hand. "See? Nothing to worry about."

"But there's also the matter of—" Jack started to object to the insane plan they'd just relayed to him, but Triss shushed him with a loud tsk.

"We'll have none of that. It'll be over before you know what's happened," she said.

Despite his continued objections, Jack was shepherded back to the *Little Princess*, which had made a tandem hyperspace jump with the *Prancer*. Alyssa and Triss settled into the cockpit of the small vessel while Jack was left in the living room. It occurred to him that he could try to make a run for it—maybe by commandeering the *Prancer*—but he'd have nowhere to go. Alyssa's crazy plan was better than no plan at all.

The ship de-coupled from the larger vessel and approached the planet. Within ten minutes, the ship began trembling as it broke through the atmosphere.

The radio in the cockpit crackled. "Unidentified craft, identify yourself."

"That's original," Alyssa muttered. "This is the *Little Princess* inbound with a prisoner for immediate incarceration," she replied, presumably over the radio.

"Name on bounty record?" the Hellana official questioned.

"Jack Tressler," Alyssa stated.

"One moment." The radio went silent for ten seconds. "Bounty confirmed. Proceed to the prisoner deposit site."

"Roger." The console beeped as Alyssa ended the call. "You're popular, Jack," she shouted back to him.

"Yipee. It feels great to be the bait..." Jack mumbled.

"There's a ninety percent chance you won't lose another eye, so you really shouldn't worry," Alyssa said.

"A whole ninety percent? Thanks, that makes me feel much better."

The vibrations intensified as the shuttle descended into the atmosphere, the small craft at the mercy of the super-heated air currents influenced by the planet's volcanic activity. Jack held onto the couch using hidden handholds beneath the cushions since there wasn't a proper restraint system. Many uncomfortable minutes passed as Triss fought to maintain control of the vessel.

Finally, they made it to the calmer air surrounding

the valley that contained the prison facility.

Moments later, a light bump indicated that they were on the ground. The engines wound down.

Alyssa and Triss came out from the cockpit.

"Stay quiet and wait for the signal," Alyssa said, approaching Jack. She pulled out the metal implement she'd previously used to adjust Jack's cybernetic and cycled it to the electromagnetic field setting, per their plan.

The enhanced vision on his left and normal on his right gave him a headache. "Got it."

Triss pulled out a pair of handcuffs from a cabinet while Alyssa prepped for debarkation. When the cuffs were in place on Jack's wrists, Alyssa released the final seal on the main hatch.

A wave of oppressive heat flooded into the cabin, burning Jack's lungs when he took his first breath of the scorched air. "Are we seriously going out there?"

"It'll just be a few minutes. You won't die," Alyssa said. She stepped outside and then immediately back in. "Okay, this *is* pretty awful."

"We can't leave the door open or everything is going to melt. Come on!" Triss said and directed Jack outside.

It was even hotter outside the ship, with a breeze that felt more like bands of heat radiating from a bonfire. Jack was pretty sure his shoes were melting on the black rock of a historical lava flow as he was guided across the open ground toward a door set into a rock outcropping in the center of the valley. The towering walls of the valley cast shadows that were likely the only reason the party wasn't instantly vaporized.

When they were five meters away, the door in the rock cracked open and a figure wearing a thermal suit poked their head outside. "Is that Jack Tressler?"

"Yes. He's here to trade places with Finn McGloven," Triss stated.

The hooded figure looked Jack over. "That doesn't

seem right."

Triss sighed loudly. "I thought this had been cleared with management? Gah, this always happens."

"Our communication relays burn out, like, *all* the time," the figure stated. "Maybe it came through while the network was down. Come on in and we'll get this sorted out."

Triss beamed. "You're the best! You know how things are with these outlaws—it doesn't really matter which one of them is locked up."

"You're telling me. Our funding is just based on the number of live bodies we have—doesn't really matter who," the guard agreed. "I'm sure the Warden wouldn't mind mixing things up with some fresh meat to roast."

"Great!" Triss nodded.

She nudged Jack forward and they passed through the partially opened doorway, followed by Alyssa.

Inside was moderately cooler than out in the open, but still far above a livable temperature by most standards.

The figure that had greeted them removed the thermal suit, revealing an oafish man with reddened skin. "You know, we don't get all that many trades."

Alyssa nodded. "It was kind of a strange order for us, too. But I guess they decided that Finn was an okay guy and ol' Jack here was a trouble-maker."

"I am," Jack stated.

Triss kneed him in the back of his leg. "Thinks himself rather witty, too."

"Well, a day in the sun would change that," the guard said. "Well, uh, let me go talk to the Warden and see if we can find any record of the trade request."

"Great! You're the best," Triss exclaimed with exaggerated enthusiasm.

The guard wandered off down the hall.

As soon as he rounded a bend, Alyssa turned to Jack.

"All right—where's the control conduit?"

Jack scanned around the hall, focusing on the image conveyed by his left eye. A glowing electrical conduit came forward through the wall. He pointed to it. "Over there."

"I need it to be a lot more precise than that," Triss said. "Show me. Hurry!"

He ran over to the wall and used his hands to trace the outline of a segment of the conduit. Triss made some markings on the wall.

"All right, stand back," she said. She slipped a metal rod with a trigger on one end out from along her thigh. In one motion, she jammed the rod into the wall.

Jack's vision lit up with a bright electrical charge as the rod made contact with the interior wires.

Triss depressed the trigger on the end of the rod and clipped on a control panel that she'd been carrying in her inner coat pocket. She made a series of furious entries. "Okay, I'm in. Locating Finn now." She scanned over the search results. "Got him. And... unlocking."

"How is he going to make it up here?" Jack asked, even though he'd tried to ask during the planning session.

Like before, Triss' answer was the same, "You don't know Finn."

"What are you doing?" The words came from down the hall deeper into the facility.

Jack looked over to see that the guard had returned with an older man, who'd been the one to speak.

"Well, they got here a lot faster than I expected," Triss muttered.

Alyssa pulled out an electrified nightstick from under her coat. "Change of plan."

CHAPTER 7

JAILBREAK

— — —

"WHAT are you doing?" the older man—whom Jack assumed was the Warden—repeated.

"Just picking up a friend. Don't mind us," Alyssa replied with a charming smile.

"Get reinforcements!" the Warden shouted to the guard.

The guard hesitated. "Well, Tony is on break, and Alberto is out sick. Robby would probably help out but he's having troubles with his lady and has been pretty distracted. And Brian? Well, Brian is just lazy."

The Warden stared at him with disbelief. "That's probably the most honest statement I've ever heard."

The guard shrugged. "I try."

"Hey guys!" someone else called from down the hall.

"Hey, Finn. Just finishing up here," Triss said. She returned her attention to the Warden. "So, we're going to take our friend and we'll be on our way."

"Not so fast," the Warden growled. "We'll—"

The guard ran away down the hall, sidestepping

Finn.

"—*I'll* stop you!" the Warden completed. He un-holstered a laser pistol strapped to his hip.

Alyssa lunged toward him.

The Warden fired, but Alyssa made an acrobatic tumble and tackled him. The laser pistol flew out from his hand and he was knocked to the floor with his head gripped between Alyssa's thighs. She flipped him to his stomach and looped his arms at the elbows using her nightstick.

"Like I said, we're just here to pick up a friend," Alyssa said with a victorious smile. "How you doin', Finn?"

"Fine and dandy," Finn replied, jogging up to them. His brown hair was swept back in a stylish wave on the top of his head, and he had a lively spark in his green eyes, despite his time spent incarcerated. "I see your hacking is still as good as ever, Triss."

"This was child's play." Triss snorted.

"And who's this?" Finn asked after looking Jack over. "And what in the planets happened to his eye?"

"Morine got creative," Alyssa said.

"It has all these cool settings!" Jack chimed in.

"Well, you look like a monster," stated Finn.

Jack shrugged. "I'm just embracing it."

Finn nodded. "You know what? Good for you. Not everyone could have your kind of confidence while looking like that."

Jack smiled. "Thanks!"

"You're all a special kind of crazy," the Warden muttered from between Alyssa's knees.

"Yeah, we like it that way," she replied. "So, we're gonna go now."

"All right," the Warden agreed.

"Cool." Finn headed for the main door.

Alyssa got up off the Warden and Triss pulled her rod

from the wall. Jack wandered out after them as the Warden waved goodbye.

Jack shook his head. "Huh. That really was surprisingly easy."

"Yeah, this place talks a big game but it's *really* poorly managed," Triss said. "A little light hacking is all it takes to catch them off-guard. This is the fourth time we've done this and they have done *nothing* differently."

Alyssa sighed. "Good help is so hard to find these days."

The four of them dashed across the tarmac as quickly as possible in the oppressive heat. Triss had to use her rod to enter in the access code for the hatch, as the hull had heated up too much without the shield up to touch with bare hands. The door swung down and they ran up the ramp, then re-sealed the door.

"Air conditioning. Now," Alyssa said while running into the cockpit to initialize the ship's systems.

"Ahh, it's good to be free!" Finn cheered while stretching his arms wide. "Thanks for coming for me, Triss. It's good to see you."

"You really need to stop getting yourself arrested," his friend replied.

"No risk, no reward. I couldn't possibly stop having fun now."

"You can continue your fun. In fact, please do," Triss clarified. "Just get better at being sneaky about it."

"You know I have a flair for the flamboyant." He preened his hair. "That said, this jumpsuit does nothing for my figure."

"We'll get you something fabulous," Triss assured him. "But first, we need to steal a nano induction module."

Finn raised an eyebrow with interest. "Taking on the Winkelson Brothers, eh?"

"We'll distract them, but we need you to crack their safe."

Finn stroked his chin. "They have an Anticrack 9000—top-of-the-line auths. They say they're unbreakable."

"And what do you say?" Triss asked.

He grinned. "What's my cut?"

"Ten percent."

He nodded thoughtfully. "Give me five minutes with it and you'll have all their goodies."

"What's *my* cut?" Jack interjected.

Triss crossed her arms. "Uh, not being dead?"

"Well, I'm risking my life now being here," Jack said. "I lost an eye—"

"And got a pretty sweet new one," she cut in.

"Still, I think I've earned my keep. I've done everything you've asked of me."

Alyssa returned from the cockpit. "He has. I think we should cut him in. What better way to motivate performance?"

"Threat of death can be pretty motivating," Triss pointed out.

"Still," Alyssa continued, "he's right. He's in this as much as the rest of us now. With the *Luxuria* destroyed, we're not under Svetlana's thumb."

"Can he be trusted?" Triss looked him over. "Trent is still looking for us. I wouldn't put it past him to send a spy."

Jack raised his eyebrow. "Trent? Never heard of him."

"If you were his spy, it's not like you'd tell us." Triss sighed.

"Honestly, I don't think he's a good enough liar to pull that off," Alyssa said. "And that's not how Trent operates. I think Jack's about as honest as they come in this trade."

Triss sighed. "All right, he can be part of the team."

Finn frowned. "I have to share my room, don't I?"

Alyssa smiled. "I'm sure you'll be best buddies in no time."

Jack clasped his hands. "Great! Do I get ten percent, too?"

The three others exchanged glances. "How about five?" Alyssa offered.

Jack shrugged. "Is there any room for negotiation?"

"No," the others declared in unison.

"Then I'll take it!"

"Excellent," Alyssa nodded. "Now go get settled in. We have a long trek ahead of us."

Jack and Finn headed down the hall toward the sleeping cabin.

Finn placed his hand on Jack's shoulder. "So, this would probably be a good time to tell you about my night terrors."

———

As it turned out, Finn's night terrors were more terrifying for observers than they were for him to experience.

Jack spent the next six hours huddled at the back of his bunk with a blanket pulled up to his chin while Finn cycled through a pattern of sounds consisting of a barking dog, a parrot imitation asking "who's your daddy?", whistlings, and a snore reminiscent of someone with sleep apnea. At several points, Jack attempted to leave the room to go sleep on the couch in the common area, but whenever he crept from his bunk Finn's eyes would open and he'd stare unblinkingly at Jack. If Jack made any move toward the door, Finn would begin to snarl. Fearing for his life, Jack would ultimately cave and return to his safe place on the lower bunk. The cycle would then reset.

After six hours, Finn stretched on the top bunk and hopped out of bed. "That was a refreshing sleep!" He noticed Jack rocking himself back and forth. "What's wrong with you?"

"Your terrors, they're..."

"Oh, yeah, I've heard it can be kind of wild. Don't worry, I won't bite."

"It certainly didn't seem that way."

Finn shrugged. "I've only drawn blood once. Anywho, we have some loot to steal!"

Jack hauled himself off the bed and followed Finn out into the common area. Alyssa and Triss were seated on the couch.

"You look like you've been up all night," Alyssa commented to Jack when she saw him.

"That's pretty accurate." Jack tousled his blond hair.

"Well, let's get you some coffee," Alyssa offered, rising from the couch to head for the galley along the opposite side wall. She poured him a mug from a metal pot and handed it to him.

Jack cradled the mug in his hands. "Thanks"

"I should really call it 'caffeine water' rather than coffee," Alyssa said with a scowl.

He sniffed the liquid in the cup. "Smells... coffee-ish."

"Alyssa is something of a coffee connoisseur," Triss chimed in.

"I'm homing in on the perfect space brew," Alyssa said with a committed glint in her eyes. "I'll have it perfected soon."

Finn groaned. "Oh stars, you're not still after vapor fusion conversion, are you?"

"It's possible! You'll see!" Alyssa declared.

"What's this now?" Jack asked.

Finn shook his head. "Alyssa got this crazy idea that it'd be possible to brew coffee using a fusion reaction directly between the coffee bean and water. It has no basis in science."

"With enough energy it's possible!" she insisted.

Finn laughed. "Maybe with a micro energy core, if those were real—oh wait. We're not stealing the MEC prototype for Svetlana to manufacture weapons, are we?"

Alyssa's face contorted into a power-hungry grin. "After we have that core, we're going to start our own empire of Spacecups."

CHAPTER 8

ADVENTURES IN FOOD SERVICE

— — —

"I have to say that working as a barista wasn't one of my career goals," Finn began.

"No, don't you see?" Alyssa continued. "We have the perfect team to get this venture off the ground. Once we have the MEC, there'll be nothing to stop us."

"I told you not to jump too far ahead," Triss cautioned. "We won't even know if your brewing method works until we get the MEC."

"It'll work, and it'll make us richer than any amount of arms dealing ever could." Alyssa's tone was one of complete confidence. "I mean, it's a highly addictive, legal drug. That's business gold right there."

"She does have a good point," Jack admitted.

"And this cut we talked about earlier—that's actually for a share in the business?" asked Finn.

Alyssa nodded. "Exactly. When the company takes off, we're all going to be billionaires."

Jack got a sinking feeling in his chest. "So when you said my money troubles would be over..."

"Yep! Five percent shareholder in Spacecups."

"What's the ROI on that? Because... debts," Jack asked tentatively.

"We should have positive cash flow and be paying dividends in two years, tops."

"Yeah..." Jack looked down. "Any chance I can get an advance on that?"

"We'll talk about it later," Triss said. "Right now, we need to get ready for our meet and greet with the Lords of Doom. They have an urgent soup delivery headed their way."

The team ate a quick breakfast and then ran over the details of the plan for the day. Jack was once again not pleased with being cast in a questionable supporting role, but like other recent events, he decided to just go along with it. Admittedly, he rather enjoyed being part of a successful op after years of failure on his own.

Four hours later, everything was ready. They executed the hyperspace jump to take them to the Winkelson Brothers' outpost at a station orbiting a red dwarf.

As they neared the station, Jack stared out the window in the common room at the cylindrical structure. "They're really out in the middle of nowhere, aren't they?"

"Adds to the mystique," Triss commented from the cockpit. "If anyone bothered to come out here, I don't think the brothers would be in business for long once they saw what the operation was really like."

"I guess we'll be the ones to officially ruin their image," Finn observed. "But, we get to become legends in the process."

"See? That'll give us all sorts of street cred for Spacecups," Alyssa chimed in.

"Taking out black market dealers and coffee are not the same thing." Finn sighed.

Jack considered it. "Well, black market, black coffee...

It might—"

"Don't encourage her!" Triss pleaded. "Let's get the MEC before we plan out a whole business for something that may not even be chemically possible to do."

Alyssa sighed. "You'll see. You'll all see!"

"Shh, time to call them," Triss said and waited for everyone to stop muttering responses to Alyssa's declaration under their breaths. She opened a comm channel to the station. "Chili delivery for the Lords of Doom."

"You're not our normal delivery person," a man said after ten seconds.

"Filling in for a friend," Triss said. She paused, then resumed with a breathy tone, "I really need the money. If there are any extra services I can provide while I'm here, do let me know."

A response came almost immediately. "We'll open the bay door for you."

"You know, things are *way* easier when you just ask to be let in rather than trying to be all sneaky-like," Jack commented when the comm channel was closed.

"It's kind of ridiculous, isn't it?" Triss replied. "I mean, half the hacking I do these days is just pretending to be an IT person and asking people to verify their password."

"That works?" Finn asked with a raised eyebrow.

"Almost every time. Believe me, I'm still stunned."

"Well, we'll have to put on a good front here," Alyssa reminded everyone. "The delivery needs to look completely legit until they open the soup containers."

"What's the trigger for the detonation?" Finn asked. "I think I was zoning out when you went over it before."

"I have a remote trigger set up," Alyssa told him. "Duck when I do."

"Sounds good." Finn nodded.

The ship pulled into the cargo bay on the space

station and the engines wound down.

Jack took a deep breath to center himself in preparation for the upcoming encounter. He slipped on a generic workman's jumpsuit over his trademark black jacket and gray pants—both to hide his holstered laser pistol and to protect his clothing against the upcoming soupy mess. Around the room, the others were donning similar apparel.

"This fabric is itchy," Triss complained as she zipped hers up, leaving the top undone to reveal just enough cleavage to keep things interesting.

"They were on super deep discount," Alyssa replied. "I think they may have been used at a fiberglass manufacturing plant."

Finn frowned. "This is what we get for trying to operate on a budget."

"You can take it off soon. Come on." Alyssa unsealed the hatch and led the way outside.

The hangar was a cavernous space of matte steel and pulley systems for maneuvering large cargo. The edges of the room were stacked with various crates and barrels that had questionable styling and were likely overpriced.

Alyssa allowed Triss to take the lead as the four of them stepped into the center of the hangar where two girthsome men were waiting for them. It didn't take long for the scent of stale sweat and fermented peppers to waft over, but everyone managed to maintain a neutral expression.

Triss put on her most charming smile and swayed her hips as she walked. "Hello, there. I'm glad we could work out a docking arrangement."

"Oh, I'll show you docking maneuvers any time you want," the slightly thinner man on the right, Don, stated as he undressed Triss with his eyes.

"I'm an excellent pilot," Bill added.

Jack resisted a gag reflex as a he watched the scene

unfold.

Triss' lips curled into an alluring smile. "Well, let me show you the goods."

She sauntered toward the cargo hold in the side of the *Little Princess*—barely large enough to transport the two soup barrels, but sufficient to suit their present purposes.

Alyssa and Finn opened the compartment on cue and rolled the barrels on their bottom edge until each was lined up on the deck in front the craft. They then stacked several down pillows next to the barrels, which had been stashed at the back of the hold.

The two men scowled as they approached the cargo.

"What are those?" Don asked as he eyed the stack of fluffy, white objects.

"Pillows," Alyssa replied, standing akimbo in an attempt to emphasize her assets hidden beneath the jumpsuit.

"We didn't order any pillows," Bill stated.

Triss flipped her red hair. "Well, maybe we can find some use for them." She leaned over one of the soup barrels and slowly unclasped the lid, making occasional eye contact with the men as she did so. "I imagine you want to give it a taste." She flipped the lid over onto the other barrel and stepped back.

Still watching Triss, the brothers approached the soup barrel, unaware that the members of the *Little Princess'* crew were inching away from them. When the brothers were just about to lean over to take a taste of the chili, Alyssa flipped the hidden trigger.

Soup rocketed into the air and showered the brothers. They yelped with surprise as the chunky, orange liquid coated them from head to foot.

Bill toppled sideways and landed on the pile of pillows. Due to intentionally weakened seams, the impact caused the pillows to explode into a cloud of down. The feathers settled on top of the soup already coating him, resulting in a horrifying impression of a snow-covered golem.

Triss gasped with feigned surprise. "Oh no! There must have been some residual carbonation from the packaging process. These eruptions almost never happen." She looked down at her jumpsuit. "I got all dirty." She ran her finger through a blob of chili on her bosom.

The brothers lay on the ground in stunned silence for twenty seconds before Don rose awkwardly to his feet. "It... burns."

Triss gave a cutesy shrug. "Well, you did order it extra spicy."

Bill rolled side-to-side until he had enough momentum to make it to his stomach. He rose to his feet using the barrel for help. "I have to clean up."

"Here, I'll help you." Triss walked with them across the hangar, leaving a trail of soupy footprints across the metal deck. As they passed through a door in the wall, she made a quick nod toward the others then disappeared.

"Okay, let's move!" Alyssa said, stripping off her outer jumpsuit.

"You know, it would have been a lot easier if we just stunned them," Jack muttered, peeling off his own jumpsuit. Fortunately, the subpar fabric appeared to have been effective at keeping his other clothes clean.

Alyssa nodded. "Yes, but A, this is more fun for Triss to lead them on, and B, rather than immediately knowing there's a problem, this way it will likely take days for them to notice. Safes aren't something that most people access every day."

"And what if they have security cameras and watch us having this conversation and then cracking the safe?"

"Fair point," Alyssa conceded. "But... exploding soup."

"That was a pretty good move," Jack admitted.

"Clock's a tickin'!" Finn shouted and ran toward the far side of the hangar.

Jack followed him, and Alyssa stayed behind to keep watch on the *Little Princess* and prepare for a quick getaway. As he ran, Jack noticed that while his clothes were clean there was a slight squishing in his shoes.

CHAPTER 9

PETTY THEFT... AND FELONIES

— — —

THE safe was behind a rather tasteful nude painting in a cluttered office at the top of a staircase down a corridor through two doors in the general direction of the center of the space station. Due to its less than accessible location, Jack and Finn were fairly confident that the Winkelson Brothers rarely accessed the room—namely due to the staircase and narrow nature of the halls.

"Time me! I want this to go down on record," Finn said as he pulled out a hand-held electronic device and a vaguely stethoscope-looking apparatus from under his jacket. He placed the end of the stethoscope-thingy on the door of the safe with the electronic pad below it.

Finn began running through combinations on the pinpad to the safe while watching the results on the electronic readout.

Jack was curious about what he was doing but decided that it was an inappropriate time to ask questions.

Speaking of time, he realized he'd never started a

counter and actually had no means of doing so. For lack of anything else, he began counting 'one-thousands' in his head. Unfortunately, he got distracted at twenty-seven and needed to guess how long he was daydreaming about eating a warm cup of chili. A similar incident happened at one-hundred-thirteen when he was overcome with a really bad itch on his ankle. He had just reached two-hundred-sixty two when Finn let out a victorious shout.

"Done!" The safe hissed open. "What's the count?"

"Uh..." Jack tried to add up the various chunks of unaccounted time. "Three hundred seconds...?"

"Wrong! Two-hundred ninety-two. There's an electronic counter here; I just wanted to keep you distracted."

"Honestly, I thought I'd be way further off," Jack admitted. "There were some... incidents."

"Yeah, that itch seemed like it was going to do you in for a few seconds there."

"You noticed that?"

Finn grinned. "I miss nothing. Like, for instance, that there's a pressure plate under these modules."

Jack turned his attention to the interior of the safe. Two dozen nano induction modules—he estimated that to be a street value of well over ten million credits—were resting on a telltale plate that was almost certainly wired into a security system. What that system would do when activated was a complete mystery.

"How do we counter it?" he asked.

Finn examined the equipment. After a moment he grinned. "Duck tape."

"Duck tape?"

The thief nodded. "I mean, the pressure plate just needs to be immobilized. The idiots have it completely depressed, so we just need to strap it down snug and throw some books on top of it. Should be fine."

"Oh. That's easy."

"Well yeah... look around. The 'Lords of Doom' pretty much half-ass everything, aside from their meal schedule. They bought a top-of-the-line safe and called it good."

"You cracked it pretty quickly," Jack pointed out.

"But I'm Finn McGloven, King of Safecracking, Breaker of Locks, the Unjailed, Father of... hopefully no one I don't know about."

Jack smiled. "Kind of egotistical to read off your own titles, isn't it?"

"And this is why everyone should have a squire," Finn grumbled while pulling some of the adhesive tape from his bag.

"Wait, you have duct tape with you?"

Finn stared at him. "Well yeah. You mean you don't always have a roll on you? And I think you intended to say 'duck tape'."

"No..." Jack replied. "Actually—"

The other man placed a finger on Jack's lips. "Shh. This explains so much." He set about his work. In a matter of two minutes, Finn had slathered on enough tape over the pressure plate that it would be able to withstand the force of a rocket blast. Just for good measure, he grabbed some metal blocks that happened to be in the corner of the cluttered room and placed them behind the rack of nano induction modules, sliding the two trays of electronic chips forward out of the safe as the blocks were put in place. Everything seemed to be fine.

"Well done, partner!" Finn said as he closed the safe and removed his cracking equipment.

Jack was just about to reply when sounds of laser pistol fire sounded in the distance.

"At least it wasn't us," Jack said with a shrug.

"There is that," Finn agreed.

They scooped up the two trays and made a run for the door, each drawing a laser pistol in their free hand.

At a full sprint, they raced down the staircase and through the corridor leading back into the hangar. When the open room came into view, Jack saw that Alyssa had taken cover behind the soup barrels and Triss was behind a crate midway between the *Little Princess* and the door where she'd left with Don and Bill. They were firing at five men in various positions around the hangar.

"Time to join in the fight," Finn said a moment before he skidded across the floor to seek cover behind a stack of crates. He got off two shots at a man crouched in a catwalk near the ceiling of the hangar.

The man pretended like he'd been hit—clutching his shoulder—then laughed and fired back at Finn.

Jack took the opportunity to run behind a crate near Finn, then onto another one several meters from Alyssa.

"What happened?" he called out to her, joining in her fire against two men behind a grouping of barrels near the door Triss had used.

"Apparently none of us bothered to ask how many brothers were in the Winkelson family," she replied, pulling her head behind the cover just as a laser blast whizzed by. "The answer is seven, by the way."

"Ah, yeah. Should have thought of that." Jack reached around the corner to fire at the shooter to the right of the door.

"Hindsight, right?" Alyssa fired three times and one shot finally connected with the left shooter.

The man collapsed on the floor, motionless.

Seeing his fallen brother, the right shooter began firing blindly toward Alyssa and Jack.

Alyssa sprayed laser fire in his general direction and the man ducked down, giving Jack the opportunity to aim. He took a headshot and the beam connected.

"Help Triss," Alyssa said while checking the charge on her pistol. "I'm almost out. I'll get the ship warmed up."

"I'll cover you." Jack targeted the men who had Triss

pinned down while Alyssa darted alongside the *Little Princess* toward the main hatch.

When she was safely inside, Jack dove for a crate closer to Triss. It didn't offer much cover, but it afforded much better sight lines to the two gunmen.

"I'll take the guy on the left," Jack called to her while gently cradling the rack of modules in the crook of his left arm.

"Got it," Triss replied, shifting her attention to the right shooter. She fired four rapid shots and the man went down.

Jack was lining up a kill shot of his own when his target suddenly dropped dead with a singed hole through his forehead.

Surprised, Jack looked to his left to see Finn standing in the open with his pistol raised in one hand and the nano induction modules tucked in the other.

"Way to steal the glory," Jack groaned and rose from the hiding place.

Finn grinned. "I'm a showoff, what can I say?"

CHAPTER 10

THE BEST LAID PLANS

— — —

WITH their foes vanquished, Triss, Finn, and Jack joined Alyssa in the common room of *Little Princess.*

"Where did things go sideways?" Jack questioned once the main hatch was sealed.

"Well, it started out okay," Triss replied. "Until I noticed the third brother."

"That would be a good clue things weren't going to plan," Jack agreed.

Triss sighed. "In retrospect, this was a terrible plan."

Jack couldn't help but make an I-told-you-so eye roll. "Didn't I say that, Alyssa?"

Triss let out a long breath. "Anyway, on our way to the shower we ran into the third brother—the first of several we didn't know would be here. I tried to work my charms on him, but either I'm not his type or the three-way competition wasn't going to work. At any rate, that's when the third brother—whose name was Derek, I guess—took out a radio to call up the other four. That's when I knew things were really off, so I faked twisting my ankle to buy some time."

"Oh, not that routine…" Alyssa groaned.

"Well, it was very effective," Triss shot back. "Derek held off on calling the other brothers, which gave Finn the time to crack the safe. We may even have been able to get the modules back on the ship without anyone being the wiser if it weren't for their stupid gerbil."

Everyone except Jack nodded solemnly.

"Figures they'd have one," Finn said.

"Am I missing something?" Jack asked. "What about a gerbil?"

"Gerbils are known to be very protective of their human caretakers," Alyssa explained. "They have an uncanny ability to detect ill-intent and will go to great lengths to warn about an impending double-cross." She returned her attention to Triss. "Lemme guess—it started barking?"

Triss nodded. "Yep."

"Barking, huh?" Jack's brow furrowed.

"Well, it's more of a soft cooing," Triss clarified. "But anyway, my cover was blown. So, I knocked Don's and Bill's heads together and started a firefight with Derek."

"What happened to Don and Bill?" Finn asked.

She shrugged. "Not sure. Derek and I ran out here shooting at each other, where the remaining brothers joined in the fun. You know the rest."

Alyssa frowned. "So, that means…"

The *pew-pew* of laser pistol fire sounded in the hangar outside as the shots struck the *Little Princess'* hull.

"They're awake," Triss completed everyone's thoughts aloud.

"Time to go!" Alyssa dashed to the cockpit with Triss.

Jack and Finn braced on the couches.

"I do feel a little badly about killing their brothers," Finn admitted. "I've always been more of a thief than a murderer."

"For what it's worth, they would have killed you if you hadn't," Jack told him.

"I know, but we broke into *their* station. Of course they'd try to defend it."

The ship's engines hummed and it lifted off the ground. Laser blasts continued to bombard the hull outside.

"Uh oh, Finn isn't getting all remorseful, is he?" Alyssa called out from the cockpit.

"A bit, yeah," Jack replied.

Triss groaned. "This happens every time. Just tell him about the Plot Device Principle."

"The what?" asked Jack.

"It's a term I coined just now," Triss continued. "Life would be pretty boring if everything always went according to plan." With that, she activated the main laser array on the *Little Princess* and cut a hole in the side of the cargo bay.

Everything not tied down was sucked across the floor toward the new opening, including Don and Bill.

"Oops. Did I do that?" Triss stopped firing.

Alyssa directed the ship toward the hole. "And *that's* how you make an exit."

The ship passed through the opening with almost no room to spare, but Alyssa's precision piloting got them clear of the station and the random pieces of cargo drifting out into space following the rapid decompression.

"Okay, so everyone's dead," Jack stated. "What do we do about the station? Someone is going to stop by for a delivery or something eventually, and we didn't exactly make any effort to hide our presence."

"That's a good point," Finn realized. "I really don't want to go back to prison."

"Uh guys…" Alyssa began slowly. "I don't think that's

going to be an issue."

Jack and Finn ran into the cockpit to look out the front window at a massive Vorlox ship posturing over the Winkelson Brothers' space station.

"Where'd they come from?" Jack wondered aloud.

"An excellent question," Finn replied, "but I suggest we don't stick around to ask."

"I'm with Finn." Alyssa activated the hyperspace drive.

The engines whined in preparation for the jump and then made a sad sputter followed by a clunk.

"We're not in hyperspace," Finn observed.

"You think?" Alyssa's hands raced over the controls as she brought up systems reports in an attempt to identify the problem.

"I think I know what's wrong." Jack gestured at the containment net that had been cast around the *Little Princess*.

Alyssa paused her work. "Yeah, that would do it."

"Is there any way out?" Finn asked.

Triss grimaced. "Nothing that might not leave us in a worst position than we're in now."

Before anyone could offer further commentary, the radio crackled to life. "We have your friends. We know you're after the MEC," a gravelly, male voice growled.

Alyssa paled. "What do you want?"

"The MEC, same as you," the Vorlox representative replied. "Bring it to us and your friends will live."

"We need proof of life," Alyssa continued. "Live video, now."

The line muted for ten seconds. "Very well," the Vorloxian conceded.

Several moments later, an incoming video request came through on the front HUD and Alyssa accepted. Jack and Finn crammed into the cockpit, huddling around the back of her chair to see.

Onscreen, Svetlana and a dozen women were seated cross-legged on the floor of what appeared to be a dormitory.

"Svetlana! Are you okay?" Alyssa asked as soon as she saw her.

"Could be worse," the other woman replied. "Mostly just pissed about the *Luxuria* getting all shot up."

"Did everyone make it out?" Triss asked.

Svetlana didn't reply at first. "Just do what the Vorlox are asking."

"You always told us never to negotiate lives, no matter what," Alyssa countered.

"This is different," Svetlana insisted. "The Vorlox aren't—"

The video cut out and the original voice stated, "You have proof of life. Your friends won't be harmed if you bring us the MEC."

"We don't have it yet," Triss stated.

"You have two days" The radio disconnected.

Out the window, the Vorlox ship fired six blasts from the oversized lasers mounted on the side, which annihilated the remains of the space station.

"There goes our physical evidence problem," Jack said.

The enemy ship maneuvered away from the wreckage and jumped to hyperspace in a flash.

Alyssa stared out the window, her face drawn with worry. "What would the Vorlox want with the MEC?"

"What *wouldn't* they want with it?" Triss countered. "They could use it for anything from a weapons system to powering a biosphere."

"Has anyone else noticed that they seem really organized and have great tech for being supposedly radiation-crazed people?" Jack observed.

"I do have to agree—this encounter did not support my previous impression of them or their reputation,"

Alyssa agreed.

"Yeah, aside from being a little trigger-happy with their laser array, they seemed pretty rational." Triss thought for a moment. "What do we really know about them?"

"The trigger-happiness isn't an isolated incident," Alyssa said. "At least five other space stations have reportedly been taken out by them in the last several months."

"You might shoot me for saying this," Jack began cautiously, "but were there criminals operating those space stations? Don't get me wrong, you're—we're—not the bad kind of criminals, but what we're doing isn't exactly legal, either."

Triss was about to punch him in the arm but Alyssa stopped her. "You might be onto something, Jack. I knew of the stations that were targeted because they were known black market trade posts for weapons and defense tech."

"With the exception of the GiganCorp research center," Triss pointed out.

"Maybe it's all connected. Who knows?" Finn speculated.

Alyssa pursed her lips. "Svetlana was starting to say something about the Vorlox not being something."

" 'Who they seem', maybe?" Triss completed.

Alyssa shrugged. "As good a guess as any."

"Then who are they really?" Jack questioned.

"I don't know," Finn cut in, "but we have two days to deliver the MEC to... somewhere. They didn't actually tell us. But if we're going to have it in-hand by then, we need to get going."

"He's right. We have a mission to finish." Alyssa turned back around in her chair to face the controls. "Now that we have the nano induction modules, we need to mine some thorium and get to the GiganCorp lab ASAP."

"Right, the part where go play with glowing green rocks..." Jack muttered.

"Oh, it's barely radioactive. We just need a slight trace."

Jack frowned. "All the same, I really thought you were joking."

CHAPTER 11

POSITIVELY GLOWING

— — —

JACK stared with dismay at the asteroid gently tumbling through space a kilometer away. "You really weren't joking."

"Seriously, this isn't a big deal," Alyssa repeated. "Of everything we have to do for this mission, this is the easiest part."

"Famous last words," Jack muttered.

"All right! The extraction assembly is ready," Triss announced from her seat in the cockpit.

Alyssa took the controls again. "I'll bring us in. Take the shot as soon as you can—it'll be tough to hold us in position with those rocks orbiting the asteroid."

"Roger that," Triss acknowledged.

Jack took a seat in the common room and grabbed onto the handholds beneath the cushions as a precaution. Regardless of Alyssa's insistence that everything would be fine, he'd been through too many "sure bets" to believe such statements.

"This might be a little bumpy..." Alyssa warned as

she directed the *Little Princess* closer to the four-hundred-meter-long rock.

The ship shuddered as its shields were bombarded by the cloud of rocky debris and dust surrounding the asteroid. The grapple line for the extraction assembly only had a three hundred meter reach, meaning that they had to fly closer to the asteroid than any flight manual would advise. In fact, in the fifth edition of *How to Avoid Huge Spacerocks*, the author had specifically warned against the very maneuver they were attempting.

Jack's objections had been overruled, of course, because his companions were insane, by his estimation. However, they were also the competent type of insane so he had reasonable confidence they'd get out of the mission alive.

Alyssa aligned the ship above a thorium deposit using the targeting overlay on the HUD.

"A little closer..." Triss urged.

"I'm trying!" Alyssa gritted her teeth as she fought against the controls.

"Almost.... Got it!" Triss fired the extractor.

The claw-like assembly and tether shot out from the belly of the *Little Princess* and embedded in the asteroid.

"Drilling underway," Triss stated. "We need a minute and then we should be all set."

Alyssa remained focused on maintaining enough slack on the tether to keep it from prematurely ripping the assembly from the rock.

After a minute, Triss beamed. "Extraction successful! Now to reel it in." She pushed the button to activate the servos.

Nothing happened.

"That's not good," she murmured.

Alyssa groaned. "Nothing ever went wrong before you were here, Jack."

"Hey, I warned—"

"Not now!" Triss cut him off. "I can't override the servos from here. They may have been damaged in the laser fire on the station."

"How securely is the extractor connected to the cable?" Alyssa asked.

Triss nodded. "I was thinking the same thing. It should hold."

Gently, Alyssa began pulling away from the asteroid, increasing the tension on the cable connecting the ship to the container now filled with a sample of thorium.

"If we lose that sample..." Triss warned.

"I know, I know. Quiet." Alyssa's gaze darted between the readings on the HUD and out the window for visual confirmation of their position relative to the tether point. "Almost..."

The taut tether snapped free of the asteroid and whipped back toward the ship, the extraction claw still attached to the end. The metal claw crashed into the portside window of the cockpit next to Alyssa. The window held but small cracks radiated from the impact site.

Alyssa pointed the ship away from the asteroid into open space and cut the thrusters. "That was way too close."

"Someone has to go out there to retrieve the canister," Triss said. "And we should probably seal that window before the crack spreads."

"Not me!' Finn said. "Those EVA suits are too claustrophobic."

"I should monitor the servos from in here," Triss suggested.

"And I'm the pilot, so..." Alyssa looked to Jack.

"Oh man. Seriously?" Jack let out a heavy sigh.

"Let's get you suited up, come on," Alyssa said and led him to the airlock at the stern of the craft.

Dragging his feet, Jack followed her. "I hate EVA."

"New guy gets the short straw," she replied as she pulled a gold-tinted suit and helmet from a storage closet.

"This smells like bile," Jack commented when he caught a whiff of the helmet.

"There may or may not have been an incident during the last EVA." Alyssa shrugged. "I'm sure you won't notice it as soon as it's sealed up."

Reluctantly, Jack donned the suit and slipped on the helmet. Contrary to Alyssa's statement, the smell was in fact much, much worse once the suit was sealed. Nonetheless, he didn't like the idea of a crack in the window of the spaceship, so he was driven to complete the job at hand.

After securing some tools to his waist belt and performing a comm check with Alyssa, he entered the tiny airlock toward the stern of the ship and waited for the pressure to drop. When all the air had been vented, the light on the outer door turned green and he opened the hatch.

"Heading out," he said into the comm.

"Slow and steady," Alyssa said on the other end.

Jack strapped onto a lead line and connected it to an anchor outside the door. He then carefully exited the ship, hanging onto handholds that seemed far too shallow in the feeble grasp afforded with the gloves of the EVA suit.

He inched along the side of the craft, gulping as he saw the tether line for the extractor stretching out into space next to the ship. Any sudden change of direction and the line could easily pin him against the hull and slice him clean through.

First, he passed by the anchor for the tether to inspect the crack in the front portside window. It wasn't pretty, but the crack appeared to be isolated to only the outermost of the two layers of aluminum silicate glass windowpanes. He unclipped a canister of sealant from his belt and slathered it along the crack. The material oozed into the crevasse and within moments the impact site was invisible.

"Good. Now for the hard part," Alyssa said.

Jack backtracked toward the tether. Once in position next to the reel, he locked the gravity boots on his EVA suit and began bashing his fist on the reel's external control panel. The random button mashing did nothing, so he flipped out a hand crank to reel it in manually.

"You owe me a shoulder massage after this," Jack panted as he cranked the reel, trading off hands when one arm tired.

"I'll get Triss right on that. She gives amazing massages," Alyssa replied.

"I'll bet you'd know."

After seven minutes of vigorous cranking, the end of the tether was finally close. Jack slowed down as the final length of line came in, and he retrieved the canister from inside the claw. Holding the canister in his left hand, he made the final cranks to return the claw to its casing in the hull and closed the cover for the control panel.

Cautiously, he unlocked his boots and made his way back inside.

"Great job!" Alyssa praised when he was safely back in the airlock.

Jack sealed the door and began to repressurize the chamber. While he waited, he examined the material inside the canister through the transparent window in its side. "Huh. Is it supposed to be glowing like that?"

CHAPTER 12

A TASTY DETOUR

— — —

"No. No, it is not." Alyssa's concern was audible over the comm.

Jack took a closer look at the canister containing the sample they'd collected from the asteroid. He knew it was supposed to be thorium, but as far as he knew, thorium didn't glow.

"Don't take off your suit just yet," Alyssa stated. "We need to figure out what's going on."

The light blue glow emanating from the canister looked almost magical in the dim lighting of the airlock.

"It's kinda pretty," Jack commented. "What do you think it is?"

"I'm not sure…" None of the concern had left Alyssa's tone.

"What color is it glowing?" Triss asked, jumping on the comm.

"Pale blue," Jack replied. "The material itself looks to be kind of metallic white."

Triss' face appeared in the tiny porthole window in

the airlock door. "Show me."

Jack held up the canister for her to get a better view.

Her eyebrows drew together. "Uhh... that looks like actinium."

"Sounds fancy."

"Yeah, well, it's not supposed to exist on its own in nature."

Jack frowned. "That's curious."

"It's also highly radioactive. Like, super-hot radioactive."

"So it's probably bad I'm holding onto it."

"Not the greatest, no. I mean, the canister *should* contain it. And the airlock is sealed against radiation, same shielding as the hull."

Jack set down the canister near the back wall. "I don't want to be in this room with the radioactive nonsense, Triss. Let me out! Alyssa, make her let me out!"

"Okay, just hold on," Alyssa soothed. "We'll go into the sleeping cabins while the door is open. Re-seal the airlock when you're inside."

"What about my suit?"

"It'll be... fine," Triss replied. "Just toss it in the closet."

"All right..." Jack agreed.

The others ran away from the door and gave him an all-clear signal when the cabin doors were closed. He opened up the interior airlock door and re-sealed it, then stripped off the EVA suit as quickly as possible. A decontamination routine activated on the suit when it was in storage.

"That's a terrible design," he grumbled.

Alyssa, Triss, and Finn crept out from the two sleeping cabins.

"Well, this is going to make the break-in significantly more difficult," Alyssa said.

"You're welcome, by the way," Jack said.

"Yes, thank you for going out there," Alyssa acknowledged. "But seriously, though, the plan counted on a stable radioactive compound. With the grapple shot, we don't have another chance to extract what we need."

"Why did you need it?" Jack asked.

"To throw off the security sensors in the GiganCorp labs," she explained. "The presence of a radioactive substance diverts some of the resources away from normal bio-detection—like a decoy."

"Well, this would make one heck of a decoy!" Jack exclaimed.

Alyssa sighed. "Way too much. I think the entire lab would lock down as soon as something that potent was detected."

Jack thought for a moment. "What are the procedures when there's a dangerous containment breach?"

"Everyone immediately goes into secure bunkers. Emergency doors seal."

"What kind of visibility do those bunkers have to security cameras and the like?" Jack prompted.

"Not the full control center, but probably some," Alyssa replied.

"But looping footage of an empty hallway is easy," Triss cut in. "And Finn and I can bypass any lock."

"Yeah we can!" Finn cheered.

Jack grinned. "Alyssa, I think getting this actinium might be a happy accident. We can clear out the whole lab and take what we want. Be in and out before anyone really knows what's going on."

A smile slowly spread across her face. "That could work. Handling the material is going to be tricky, though. We'll need extra radiation suits."

"They probably have some stashed away at GiganCorp, right?" Triss prompted.

"Almost certainly," Alyssa confirmed. "But it's

possible all of them will be taken by staff as soon as the alarm is triggered."

Jack smirked. "Easy. We just need to make sure the alarm triggers when the facility isn't fully staffed."

"We have two days to get this done," Alyssa reminded him. "It's not like we can wait for the weekend. And overnight, the security systems follow different protocols and we'd be screwed."

"So we time it right during normal operating hours but make sure to clear it out," Jack stated.

Alyssa raised an eyebrow skeptically. "And how do we do that?"

Jack waved his hand. "By declaring a bottomless margarita happy hour at the nearest bar, of course! And 'all you can eat' taquitos for three credits. That'll empty the place."

"I'm beginning to realize that most of our ideas revolve around food," Finn observed.

Jack nodded. "I really am bummed about all of that chili going to waste earlier."

Alyssa shrugged. "Cost of doing business."

Triss had a mischievous glint in her eyes. "Jack, this idea of yours will work. Just mentioning taquitos is making me hungry."

"Me too," Finn agreed. He looked around the group. "Should we go for taquitos right now?"

"I think we need to test out the bar to make sure it has sufficient draw to serve our purposes in the plan," Alyssa said.

"Yes, just vetting the plan," Triss concurred.

"Why do I not have taquitos in my mouth *right now*?" Alyssa cried as she dashed for the cockpit.

"I'm soooo hungry now that I'm thinking about it," moaned Triss. "How far away is the GiganCorp lab with the MEC?"

"About four hours in hyperspace," Alyssa said with a

frown.

"Four hours?! I'll never make it," Finn wailed.

"We could have a snack to hold us over—" Jack started to suggest, but the others fixed dagger-eyes on him.

"Taquitos *are* a snack. An ultimate snack! We can't snack and then have another snack," Triss stated.

"You know..." Finn clasped his hands. "What if we stop off at a nearby station to have some taquitos and then go to the place near GiganCorp to get *more* taquitos?"

Alyssa's face lit up. "Finn, you are a brilliant, brilliant man."

CHAPTER 13

HIDDEN PAST

— — —

WIPING his hands on a napkin, Jack eased back onto the couch. "That was so good."

Triss reclined next to him. "I forgot how much I love taquitos."

"Must... resist... food coma..." Alyssa hauled herself out of the chair at the foldout table near the galley.

"She's right, we need to get to the system with GiganCorp's lab," Finn said from the chair across from her. "Wake me up when we're at the next taquito place."

"Must focus." Alyssa shook her head side-to-side rapidly and rubbed her eyes. "Okay, hyperspace." She plodded into the cockpit.

Triss winced and then forced herself off the couch. "I shouldn't have gotten the double portion."

"You *can* have too much of a good thing," Jack said.

"Lies." Triss followed Alyssa into the cockpit.

Jack held on to the handholds in the couch as the ship made the jump to hyperspace. The pressure during acceleration was significantly more uncomfortable than normal with his full stomach.

As much as he wanted to nap during transit—both as a result of his large meal and from being up all night thanks to Finn's bizarre night terrors—he knew there was a break-in to plan.

Alyssa left Triss in charge of piloting the ship while she helped Jack and Finn map out the details.

Jack was surprised by Alyssa's intimate knowledge of the facility. He asked dozens of random questions while they were going over the building schematics and security systems, and somehow she had a definitive response. Eventually, his curiosity got the better of him.

"Alyssa, how do you know so much about such an ultra-secure facility? I mean, I know it doesn't seem all that secure because we're talking about all the ways we can outsmart the systems, but we *are* the best."

"Well, *we're* the best. You're Jack," she countered.

"Now you're just dodging my question."

She looked down at the tabletop.

"Did you used to work there?" Jack pressed.

"Yes," she replied at last.

Finn's eyes widened. "You never told me that before! I thought you just had an in with security or something."

"No, not exactly." Alyssa hesitated. "When I left the company, my access credentials were never fully deactivated."

"That seems like a pretty big oversight," Finn commented.

"It was. Especially considering it's been seven years," she replied.

Jack eyed her. "How do you know you still have access?"

"I can still log into the VPN, which means I'm in the system. I've been regularly logging onto the account over the years to keep it from going dormant," Alyssa revealed. "The communications forwarded through that account are how I learned they'd constructed the MEC prototype."

Finn nodded thoughtfully. "That explains a lot."

"That means my old keycard should be able to help get us in through the front door," Alyssa continued. "However, since it's an old account, we'll need to trick the system."

"Hence the nano induction module," Triss supplied from the cockpit.

"Exactly," Alyssa confirmed.

"You must have had some pretty high-level security clearance if you were receiving messages about a product that hasn't been publicly announced," Jack realized.

"Yeah, you could say that." Alyssa shrugged.

Jack wasn't convinced that she was telling the whole story. "What was your job at GiganCorp?"

"What did you say, Triss?" Alyssa called out in an obvious evasion. "You need me to look at what?"

"I didn't—" Triss cut her off. "Right. The, uh, forward inertial dampeners are giving some readings slightly outside of spec. You should totally double-check that right away."

"That sounds urgent," Alyssa said and rose from the table. "I think we've gone over the important parts of the plan. We'll be there soon."

Jack and Finn exchanged bewildered glances as Alyssa retreated into the cockpit with Triss.

"That was weird, right?" Jack whispered.

"Very odd," Finn agreed in a hushed voice.

"What do you think she's hiding?"

Finn shook his head. "This is the first I've ever heard about her being a corporate employee. I've known her for about five years and in that time she's been all about skirting the law, first with Trent and then with Svetlana's crew. Frankly, I can't imagine her being one of those suits."

"Me either. And why won't she talk about it?"

"Most of us have some element of our past we'd rather forget," Finn stated.

"True enough, but that reaction... There's something she really doesn't want us to know."

Jack and Finn decided it was best to not go down the dangerous path of idle speculation, so they let the issue drop for the time being. However, Jack was committed to getting the truth out of Alyssa at the first possible opportunity.

The rest of the jump passed by quickly. Like many of the inhabited systems in the middle zone between the central worlds and outermost colonies, the system consisted of one main terraformed planet, several space stations, and a moon designated as the dumping ground for anything that wasn't wanted by the other establishments. The GiganCorp research lab was naturally situated on an equatorial continent of the planet that afforded the nicest climate and beachfront. Fortunately, being the main attraction to the planet, it was also located next to a port on the surface, and in proximity to the restaurant on which Jack's plan to clear out GiganCorp's lab hinged.

The *Little Princess* entered the atmosphere and descended to the port. Controllers directed them to a berth.

"Just a quick taste," Alyssa told everyone once they were docked. "No more double portions."

"You'll have to handle the ordering, then," Triss told her. "I don't trust myself to order responsibly."

"Me either," Finn admitted.

"I'm really not that hungry again yet," Jack ventured, but he quickly backpedaled when he saw the utter appall on the face of the others. "Kidding, of course."

Everyone relaxed.

Triss chuckled. "I was going to say... No one turns

down more taquitos!"

They secured the *Little Princess* at the port and took a moving walkway from the docking area to a commercial district. The target establishment, Mexcelente, had a front façade finished in faux stucco with sombreros and maracas painted in red, green, and blue. Synth mariachi music filled the hall.

"I smell them!" Hunger was in Triss' eyes.

"I'm ordering, remember," Alyssa told her and took the lead into the restaurant.

Several small groups were waiting in the lobby, and Alyssa needed to force her way to the front host stand.

An unenthused red-headed man wearing a fake black moustache greeted them, "Welcome to Mexcelente, home of the most mexcelente burritos. How many in your party?"

"Four," Alyssa replied.

The man consulted the holoconsole in front of him. "It'll be about a forty-minute wait for the dining room."

Triss gripped Alyssa's arm. "I can't wait that long."

"What about the bar?" Alyssa asked the host.

"Bar is open seating. Help yourself," he told them. "Next customer."

Triss forged ahead to the bar off the right side of the lobby. She spotted a tall table near the middle and beckoned everyone over.

"You really have no impulse control," Alyssa commented as she took a seat at the table.

"I'm sorry. Me and taquitos are like you and coffee," Triss said.

"I'm all for the bar seating." Finn began perusing the drink menu.

Jack settled into the final chair and looked over the main food menu. It seemed fairly typical at first, until he noticed that some of the proteins were somewhat unusual. "Frog tacos?"

"It's French-Mexican hybrid from Old Earth," Alyssa told him without looking up from her own menu.

Jack wrinkled his nose. "That's so unnatural! I think I'll stick to the synthobeef."

As he set down his menu, Jack noticed that a man was eyeing their table from across the bar. "We have company."

Alyssa glanced up and spotted the man. She immediately looked back down and tried to hide behind her menu.

The man rose from his seat and approached them. "Alyssa?"

She swore under her breath and slowly lowered the menu, forcing a smile. "Hey, Ed."

"Wow, long time no see!" Ed exclaimed. "I didn't expect to see you around these parts again."

"Well, business…" she said with a shrug.

"Huh." He nodded. "Do your parents know you're back?"

"No, and I wasn't planning to reach out to them," Alyssa stated flatly.

The man frowned. "Well, a lot of people would be happy to see you. It's not every day that the genius daughter of one of GiganCorp's leading researchers returns to town."

CHAPTER 14

TEAM BONDING

— — —

JACK and Finn openly gawked at Alyssa.

"You're the daughter of one of the GiganCorp executives?" Jack stammered.

"I'm no one," Alyssa said and got up from the table. "Don't tell anyone I was here, Ed." She started for the exit.

Triss caught her hand and drew her back. "No more running. You promised."

Alyssa let out a slow breath and returned to her seat.

Ed searched Alyssa's face. "What made you leave the company so suddenly?"

"Some matters of business aren't worth the personal sacrifice," she responded cryptically.

Jack noticed Triss squeeze her hand under the table.

"Well, sorry to have interrupted your dinner," Ed murmured. "Good to see you, Alyssa." He returned to his seat.

Finn waited until Ed was beyond earshot. "I get not wanting to explain yourself to him, but I think it's time you tell us what's really going on here."

Alyssa nodded. "I was hoping we could be in and out without running into anyone who knows me, but that was wishful thinking." She took a deep breath. "Yes, my parents work for GiganCorp, and so did my grandparents, and great-grandparents, etcetera. I went to college to study engineering, just like I was supposed to, and began working in the research division as soon as I graduated. Things were fine for a couple of years, but then Competron came into the mix."

"They're GiganCorp's main competition, right?" Finn prompted.

"Yes. Really, the *only* competition," Alyssa confirmed. "But it's not just competition in terms of the products. Competron has a fundamentally different business model—they're all about freemium business models so no one has to go without, but those with the means can get whatever they want.

"Obviously, this caused some problems in the executive ranks of GiganCorp. How could the company compete if someone else was giving away the same product for free?"

"Free is nice," Jack said.

"Exactly." Alyssa nodded. "So, being the unimaginative lot that they are, they decided to send me to Competron as a mole. That's when I learned that Competron is actually a pretty nice place to work and they have a winning mission statement and all that."

"So you defected?" Finn said.

"In a roundabout way. Triss and I met at Competron, where she was one of the engineers working on AI integration," Alyssa explained.

Understanding registered in Finn's eyes. "Ah, that's how you got so good."

"I wasn't nearly as good before I met you," Triss smiled.

Finn ducked his head bashfully. "Aw, shucks."

"Anyway," Alyssa continued. "GiganCorp wanted me to come back and spill everything I'd learned about Competron, but I wanted to stay. After some long, boring conversations about non-competes, I stumbled across a job posting on a board looking for volunteers to help the disenfranchised. I was annoyed enough with corporate interests that it sounded appealing. Things started out innocently enough, but Triss and I eventually found ourselves at the inner circle of Svetlana's little empire. After things went bad with Trent, it was too dangerous to venture out on our own, so we were stuck."

"Then this job with GiganCorp came up," Triss added. "It was a chance to take some tech that could allow a third player to enter into the competition mix in a big way."

"Through coffee?" Jack raised an eyebrow.

"That's one application," Alyssa said. "Obviously that wasn't going to be the only thing."

"But now the Vorlox are after the same thing, for unknown reasons," Finn said. "So that makes things tricky."

"It does. I still don't know their angle," Alyssa admitted. "But I do know that GiganCorp is not the company that should have sole use of the MEC," she whispered the last part so it couldn't be heard beyond their table.

"Okay, so we carry out our plan, and then...?" Jack prompted.

Alyssa shrugged. "Confront the Vorlox and find out if they're friend or foe, I guess."

"Yeah, confront the big, angry, murdery people in the giant ship with spikes and huge guns. That's a *great* plan," Jack muttered.

"They might be very nice," Triss pointed out.

Jack sighed. "Yeah, sure..."

A minute later, the waiter came to take their order.

"Taquitos all around," Alyssa ordered without her

previous enthusiasm for the item.

"Single or double?" the waiter asked as she consulted her handheld touchpad.

Alyssa slumped in her chair. "Singles for them and a double for me."

"Now who's the one with self-control issues?" Triss said with a raised eyebrow.

"Comfort food," was Alyssa's only response.

"Okay, three singles and a double order of taquitos. What meat?" the waitress asked.

"Surprise us," Finn replied.

Jack's pulse spiked. "You did see the menu, right?"

Finn flipped his wrist. "Variety keeps things interesting."

"Surprise it is…" Jack conceded.

The waitress made a notation. "And anything to drink?"

"Premium margarita for me!" Finn said with a raised finger.

"No drinking. We have work to do," Alyssa objected.

"Not until tomorrow afternoon," Triss pointed out. "Everything has been prepped."

Alyssa melted when she saw Triss' pleading eyes. "All right, premium margaritas all around."

Finn grinned. "A right proper party!"

One drink quickly turned into four and the group confirmed that a bottomless margarita offer would make an excellent distraction for the GiganCorp employees. The taquitos, likewise, were suitably satiating and a nice upgrade from the budget place they'd hit up after leaving the former Winkelson Brothers' station.

With several drinks in him, Jack was feeling warm and happy even though the world was a little wobbly around him. "Guys… thanks for taking me in."

"Uh oh, I sense a sentimental speech coming on," Finn quipped.

"No, really!" Jack insisted. "Things were pretty rough after my childhood stage acting dreams didn't work out. I got involved in petty crime, and I was floundering for a long time. Deep in debt, few friends, and no one I could trust... I just wanted a fresh start. I know you were just using me at first, but over the last few days I've started to feel like one of the team—and this cybernetic eye has even grown on me."

"Well, you've grown on me, too," Alyssa gave him a gentle punch in his arm.

"Yeah, you're all right," Triss smirked.

"I vote we keep him," Finn said. His words were fairly slurred, being three drinks deeper than everyone else.

"Really?" Jack's eyes lit up. "I can stay after this mission is over?"

Alyssa shrugged. "If we're still alive, sure. You've been a good boy."

Triss reached over the table and ruffled his hair. "That's a good boy!" she said in the same tone as one might praise a dog.

Jack yanked his head away from her but secretly he didn't care. He was the new guy and a little hazing was to be expected. For once, it was nice to be part of a team.

CHAPTER 15

HAZY RECOLLECTIONS

— — —

JACK awoke with an impressive hangover. The spinning of the world around him from last night had subsided, but his head ached and his stomach felt like he'd spent all night in zero-*g*.

He assessed his surroundings and found that he was in his bed on the lower bunk in his cabin.

However, Finn was passed out half on Jack's bed and half on the floor. "Where's the cake?" he said as he woke with a start. "Ugh." He clutched his head.

Jack forced himself into a sitting position, making everything feel worse. "How many did we have last night?"

"I lost count." Finn rubbed his eyes.

"Me too. I wonder how Alyssa and Triss are doing?"

"I doubt they're up yet."

The two men slowly stood up and stumbled toward the door.

"I think I'm still a little drunk," Jack commented when he got to his feet. The world seemed like it was tilted at an angle. It was then that he realized his cybernetic eye implant had been knocked off-center. He twisted it back into position. "Never mind. Just hungover."

Finn slid the door open and they stepped into the hallway.

The scent of slightly burned coffee filled the common room. Triss and Alyssa were seated at the galley table, looking perfectly rested and refreshed.

"About time you got up," Alyssa said. "Looks like you had a rough night."

"How are you not dead?" Finn moaned. "You were matching us drink for drink."

She shook her head. "Oh, we switched to non-alcoholic daiquiris after the second round. You must have been too busy to notice, and afterward you were too drunk to have noticed much of anything."

"Should we remind them about the exotic dancers?" Triss asked.

Alyssa looked over Jack and Finn. "Maybe we better not."

"You can't make a comment like that and not elaborate!" Jack exclaimed. He winced at the sound of his own loud voice.

"You had a group of exotic dancers that took a liking to you last night," Alyssa said. "I think you went to make out in the corner for a while."

Jack nodded with satisfaction. "Was she hot?"

"Oh, you misunderstand," said with a little smile. "It was a group of men. But they were hot, yes."

Triss smirked. "They said you were pretty."

"If they called him pretty, then I must have been their god," Finn declared.

"You got as much attention as you could handle, don't worry," Alyssa said. "You wandered off to a back room for a while and I'm not sure what went on, but when you came back you looked happy. Then you tried to crash another bachelorette party."

Finn nodded. "That sounds about right."

"What do you mean 'another'?" Jack asked. "And I'm surprised I didn't zero in on the bachelorette group. That's normally my thing."

"Oh, you did," Triss clarified. "You were the center of attention with the first group."

He smiled smugly. "Oh yeah?"

Alyssa nodded. "They had a great time with you."

Realization sparked in Finn's bleary eyes. "Oh, that explains things. I was wondering..."

"Wondering what?" Jack searched the others' faces for clarification.

"Look in the mirror," Alyssa suggested.

Jack hurried to the washroom to look in the mirror over the sink. To his surprise, a fully make-upped face stared back at him, complete with false eyelashes, mascara, painted eyebrows, eyeshadow, rouge, and lipstick. With the flush on his face hidden beneath the rouge, Jack returned to the galley area. "Did this happen before or after the exotic dancers took a liking to me?"

"Before, of course," Triss said, holding in a giggle.

"You probably spent a good three hours at the bar that way," Alyssa shook her head as she chuckled. "You really have no game—just walked up to the bachelorette party sloshing the drink in your hand and babbling about rabbits, or something. They sat you down and put on your face."

"I think it kind of suits him, don't you?" Triss commented to Alyssa with a twinkle in her eyes.

Alyssa nodded. "Very striking."

Finn reached up to check his own face.

"No, you're good," Jack said. "Looks like I got all the honors this time."

"That's not all you got..." Triss snickered.

"I don't want to know." Jack returned to the

bathroom to wash up. Unfortunately, the lipstick and eyeliner proved to be one of the more permanent varieties.

By the time he was showered and dressed, his headache had receded and his stomach was much more settled. He found the others still in the galley munching on leftover taquitos. Sadly, they weren't nearly as good as when fresh. Nonetheless, he ate until he was an appropriate level of full.

"What do we do until it's time to head into the GiganCorp lab?" Jack asked.

"Charades?" Finn suggested.

While not a terrible suggestion, Jack soon regretted agreeing to the idea because the others took the game as an opportunity to mime Jack's various escapades from the previous night. The prompts included winners such as, 'Jack having one too many', 'Jack and the dancer get it on', and 'Jack being prettified'. He didn't find it nearly as amusing as the others did.

After two hours, it was time to prep for the GiganCorp break-in. While everyone geared up with what they'd need for their roles, Jack took the opportunity to practice changing the modes for his cybernetic eye using his thoughts. It took concentration and several attempts, but he found that he was able to cycle through the different settings.

By mid-afternoon, everyone was ready to head into the lab.

Jack wasn't surprised to find that he'd been nominated to carry the canister containing the actinium. Triss insisted, however, that all scans showed the canister was containing the radiation, despite their initial fears. All the same, he couldn't help feeling a little nervous carrying it in a backpack—especially since everyone else gave him a several meters buffer while they walked over to the facility.

They gathered outside the main entry gate, which presented more like the approach to a luxury beach resort than a research laboratory. Tropical trees lined a paved path and bushes with red flowers circled an elaborate three-tier fountain topped with a giant G.

"Everyone ready?" Alyssa asked.

They nodded.

"Okay. Sending the happy hour announcement now!" Alyssa said as she sent the invite via her mobile.

Three minutes passed in silence as they waited for the marketing offer to do its thing. Then, people began flooding out of the front doors.

"Bottomless margaritas?" one woman in a white lab coat was saying. "And anywhere in the restaurant—not just the bar? Wow!"

"I know, it's amazing!" her colleague replied.

Alyssa nodded with satisfaction as she did a rough headcount of those leaving. "That should clear out the lab pretty well and be enough to overwhelm the host at the restaurant. We should have a good half an hour before they realize that the pricing offer isn't real."

"And by then the smell of fried awesomeness will have captivated them." Finn got a blissful, faraway look in his eyes.

"Stay focused," Alyssa stated. "We're going in."

"That's what he said," Jack snickered.

Alyssa rolled her eyes and then led the way across the remainder of the front walkway. She confidently strode into the building lobby with the others in tow.

At the back of the lobby, two guards dressed in white body armor were seated behind a reception desk. They looked over the new arrivals.

"You don't work here," the guard on the right said.

"Yeah we do," Alyssa lied. "We were onsite at a client meeting and wearing street clothes for the day."

"Oh, okay," the guard replied.

Alyssa walked over toward the controlled access door on the left of the lobby. She stealthily placed the nano induction module over the keycard reader. "Didn't you two get the message about bottomless margaritas and three credit taquitos at Mexcelente?"

The two guards looked at each other.

"I told you we shouldn't have turned off email!" the one on the left exclaimed.

"Better hurry!" Alyssa urged while she activated the induction module to override the keycard's connection to the central database. "Everyone else is already on their way over. We're just dropped off some stuff we brought to the meeting and then we'll join you."

"Think it's okay to run over for a few minutes?" the guard on the right asked the other.

"Yeah, no one ever comes in here. It'll be fine," the left guard replied.

"Great!" Alyssa swiped her keycard over the disabled access pad. The light turned green. "See you over at Mexcelente!"

The guards rose from their desk. "See you there! Thanks for letting us know."

Jack, Finn, and Triss darted through the door before it closed, with Triss grabbing the nano induction module as she passed by.

"This security really is a joke," Jack said when everyone was on the other side and the door was closed.

"Oh yeah, it's awful," Alyssa agreed. "Hellana, 'high security' labs like this, it's all the same—perpetuate a reputation of being secure and rely on those rumors to maintain security."

"So robbing a bank..." Jack ventured.

She nodded. "Walk in and take whatever you want. Most will even give you a goody bag just for coming in."

"Done it. It's true," Finn added.

"Huh." Jack began planning his next venture.

"All right," Alyssa said, turning to the task at hand, "the radiation suits should be down here." She directed them to a side corridor. "I think it's this way..."

The interior walls were all stark white plastic panels that had a glossy sheen under the light cast from the illuminated ceiling. White tile covered the floor, and a black baseboard lined both sides, with a black cap wrapping the corners of walls at the hallway intersections to increase visibility.

"Yes, here we go." Alyssa stopped next to a section of white paneling that had an orange rim. An image of a hazmat suit was depicted on the center of the panel. "Jack, switch your vision over to the electromagnetic field mode."

He concentrated on the eye controls and saw his left field of vision switch to the desired setting. "Got it."

"Do you see any wires?" Alyssa asked.

"Yes, going from the emblem at the center up to the right edge of the case.

"Okay, now switch to infrared," Alyssa instructed. "Is there any hotspot where those wires disappear into the wall?"

"No, just blue and green," he said.

Alyssa nodded. "Excellent, so it's not wired to an alarm." She pressed the emblem on the center of the panel and the door opened. "You can go back to normal vision. That's all we needed."

"That's it?! You can't be serious."

"I meant for now, Jack. We still need the eye to mimic a retinal scan."

"But still... Why did you need to take my eye and give me this implant for *that*?" he exclaimed.

"Well, we couldn't very easily walk around with a scanner," Alyssa countered.

Jack looked down at their bags of gear. "Oh, really?"

Alyssa shrugged. "In retrospect, it probably wasn't necessary for this part. But look how useful you got to feel! And you did say the settings were cool."

"Yeah, I guess they are..." Jack admitted.

"Anyway, time is wasting," Alyssa said. She turned back to the cabinet, which contained a dozen suits in shades of yellow, green, blue, and pink. Alyssa handed Jack one of the pink suits.

He sighed and set down his backpack containing the actinium before he took it from her. "Seriously?"

"It matches your lipstick." She grinned.

Alyssa took a yellow suit for herself and gave Felix blue and Triss green. They helped each other into the awkward headpieces and checked the seals.

Once satisfied that everything was in order, Alyssa removed the actinium canister from the backpack and carried it into the main hallway. "Here we go."

She popped the seal.

Five seconds passed while they waited for the radiation signature to be detected.

An alarm blared in the hall and the lights changed to red. The alarm subsided momentarily for an automated announcement, "Radiation leak detected. Proceed to the nearest safe room and await instruction."

Their plan to empty out the facility seemed to have been effective, as they saw no one enter the hall to go to the lockdown rooms. Not having time to wait around, the group followed Alyssa further inside toward the specific lab where the prototype MEC was developed.

The main corridor was blocked by an emergency containment door.

"Time for us to earn our keep," Felix said with the grin to Triss.

They pulled out electronic equipment from a small duffle bag and tapped into the control panel next to the door. Alyssa had explained that keycards couldn't override the emergency protocols to prevent some well-meaning worker from flooding an area with radiation while trying to let someone through the door.

The sealed door proved to be no barrier for Finn's

and Triss' skills, however, and the group was soon back on their way.

Jack lost track of their path as they wound through the corridors and down several stairwells, with Finn and Triss disabling the security doors as needed.

"I can't believe you remember your way around here," Jack commented when Alyssa made yet another turn.

"I spent years here. It's difficult to forget," she replied. "Ah, here it is."

She had stopped outside a lab entrance with sliding double doors. 'Top Secret' was written in giant red lettering above the door.

"A little on the nose." Triss smirked when she read it.

"No room for ambiguity, that's for sure." Alyssa located a biometric scanner next to the door. "Okay, Jack, you're up."

"Hold still," Triss instructed, and she went to work with Finn on syncing their computers with Jack's cybernetic eye.

A minute later, they had him look into the retinal scanner. The light shone green on the lock and the doors slid open.

On the other side, a woman looked up in surprise. "Who are— Alyssa?"

Alyssa removed the hood of her hazmat suit, no longer needed so far from where they'd left the actinium. "Hi, Mom."

CHAPTER 16

HEIST

— — —

"Alyssa... care to explain?" Jack slipped off the headpiece of his own hazmat suit.

The captain let out a long breath. "Okay... So, when I said I worked here at GiganCorp, I maybe should have mentioned that I was on the team working on the MEC with my mother, Mariah, here. My father is the Director of this R&D division."

Mariah crossed her arms. "What are you doing back here, Alyssa? I thought your clearance had been revoked when you ran off with your girlfriend."

"Administrative oversight," Alyssa replied. "I see you had no trouble taking all the credit for my work."

"This was always a team effort. And you left the team," her mother replied.

Finn raised his hand. "Sorry to interrupt the family reunion, but we have a job to do."

Alyssa nodded. "He's right. Sorry, Mom, but we're going to take the MEC."

"Like hell you will! Guards will be here any moment,"

Mariah responded.

"Nope." Finn shook his head. "Everyone is busy imbibing and snacking until they realize they'll have to pay full price."

Mariah worked her mouth. "You mean you just walked in here and you think you can walk right out?"

"That's precisely what's going to happen." Alyssa headed for the back of the lab.

Three workstations in the middle of the space were filled with electronic components and a holodisplay for overlaying various digital models with the physical parts.

Jack scanned over the various components and tools scattered on the workstations, looking for anything worthy of adding to his collection of random things. A compact soldering gun caught his eye.

He reached for it. "Is that—"

"No, we're only here for one thing," Alyssa stated.

He sighed. "Fine."

The centerpiece along the back wall was a plexiglass enclosure containing a pedestal topped with a compact metallic cylinder approximately eight centimeters in length and two centimeters in diameter. Blue grooves ran the length of the sides up to the black caps on the ends.

"It looks even better in real life," Alyssa murmured as she admired it.

"You did a brilliant job with the design, I'll give you that," her mother said. "But you walked away from it when you walked away from us."

Alyssa scoffed. "This will never be used for good so long as it's with GiganCorp. You have to know that."

"It's business." Mariah shrugged. "You're the one who couldn't separate family from the day job."

"I was doing a fine job of it until you asked me to commit corporate espionage."

"So you went to work for a weapon's dealer instead? Great career move." Mariah sighed. "You could have been running this company in another ten years, Alyssa. Your vision is wasted."

"Not wasted at all," Triss interjected. "She just had a vision bigger than yours."

Mariah smiled but her eyes were narrowed. "You must be the one who caused her life to derail."

Alyssa examined the lock on the case containing the MEC. "My life is right on track, Mother. It just isn't the path you wanted for me."

"It's a real pleasure to meet you, by the way," Triss said to Mariah with thick sarcasm.

Jack could see that the situation was on the precipice of devolving into an argument about parenting techniques and child rebellion, so he elected to follow Alyssa to the back of the room and assess the case with her. "Let's get the MEC and get out of here. The restaurant could catch onto our ruse at any time," he urged.

"Right." Alyssa took a centering breath. She placed her hand on the biometric lock for the case; it let out an angry beep.

"The central security team may have overlooked your access, but I didn't," Mariah said. "You'll never—"

Finn knocked her on the back of her head with a metal frame component that had been on one of the workstations. "Sorry, Alyssa."

"No apology needed," she replied. "I was about to do that myself. Help me get her over here."

Finn and Alyssa dragged Mariah's unconscious form to the MEC's case. Alyssa grabbed her right hand and placed it on the biometric scanner. The display prompted for a password.

"Triss, a little help?" Finn said.

"On it." Triss took her hacking kit and hooked into the console. She ran through the password combinations; in a matter of seconds, a match appeared and the case unlocked. "Huh. It was 'FuzzybuttOns', apparently."

"Ah," Alyssa nodded. "Good ol' Mr. Fuzzybuttons. He was my pet rabbit."

"Oh, you never mentioned him before," Triss commented.

Alyssa scowled. "Yeah, it's a bit of sore subject."

"Why, what happened to him?" Jack asked.

"My parents decided it would be a great life lesson to eat him for dinner. Figures Mom would immortalize that event with her password."

Jack's mouth dropped open. "Your parents made you eat your pet rabbit?"

Finn whistled between his teeth. "That's some messed up parenting."

"Yeah... I'll just be the one to say it," Triss cut in. "Your mom is pretty awful."

"No need to tell me." Alyssa dropped Mariah on the floor and opened up the MEC case. She gingerly took the device from the pedestal and examined it. "I'll find a way to get this into the right hands—somewhere as far away from here as possible. We need to grab the schematics, too."

"I'm on it." Finn pivoted to one of the workstations so he could access the files and grab the relevant documentation.

Triss handed Alyssa a carrying case for the MEC. "What do we do with your mom?"

"Lock her in the closet, I guess," Alyssa suggested. "Someone will find her eventually."

Jack helped Alyssa and Triss drag Mariah to a closet on the side wall and prop her up inside. She stirred when they had her in position and then began snoring softly.

Alyssa was the last to step out from the closet when they were finished. "Maybe we can come to terms with each other eventually."

Triss took her hand. "I'll be here to support you no matter what happens."

"Thanks."

"I hate to break up the tender moment," Finn interjected, "but I have the files. And I just checked the security feed and we're about to have some company. Looks like not everyone got our email about Mexcelente, and some of the guards that stayed behind seem to have found our actinium."

"No need for the suits anymore?" Jack asked.

"Not as far as I'm concerned." Finn began removing his. "The actinium has been removed."

The others quickly stripped down to their regular street clothes and grabbed their gear.

"We'll have to make a run for it," Alyssa said. She drew her laser pistol. "And we might have to shoot our way out."

Finn readied his pistol and grinned. "Oh darn."

CHAPTER 17

THE GREAT ESCAPE

— — —

JACK followed Alyssa, Triss, and Finn out of the lab. Moments after the door slid closed behind them, rapid footsteps echoed down the hall from the direction of the exit.

"That's the only way out," Alyssa said. "If they shoot at you, shoot back."

"No need to tell me twice." Triss aimed her laser pistol in front of her.

"No argument here." Jack readied his weapon. Without the containment canister or hazmat suit, he felt nimble and ready for anything the guards could throw his way. He smiled with anticipation for the thrill of the fight ahead.

Alyssa noticed his enthusiasm. "Why don't you go first, Jack."

He groaned. "You just want them to use me for target practice instead of you."

"Obviously. Go on!" she urged.

With a sigh, he loped down the hall. "I have no idea

where I'm going, by the way."

"Follow the bad guys," Triss replied. "It's a fair bet they'll be blocking our path."

"Yay—" Jack's sarcastic retort was truncated by a laser blast zipping by his ear. "And they found us." He ducked around the corner of the nearest side corridor.

"Pretty sure they knew where we were the whole time." Alyssa slid in next to him and crouched low to the floor.

"Hand over the MEC and come out with your hands up!" a male guard called out.

"Gonna pass on that." Alyssa reached her hand around corner and opened fire.

"Take cover!" the guard ordered his companions.

Jack peeked around the corner as Alyssa pulled back, and he fired at the shoulder of someone wearing white body armor who was taking cover in the next hallway intersection. The shot connected and the guard sprawled dead on the ground.

"Nice shooting," Alyssa said. She poked her head out enough to spot a target and fired, taking out another guard.

Triss and Finn were hunkered down on the other side of the hallway intersection opposite Alyssa and Jack, and they were engaged with their own set of guards.

"We're picking 'em off!" Finn cheered. "Keep at it."

It was Jack's turn to take a shot while Alyssa planned her next move. He switched glanced around the corner, seeing one of the white-clad guards running across the hall to reposition. Jack fired two shots in rapid succession and the guard was struck in the leg and then his torso, causing him to fall backward with a cry.

"We'll have them in no time," Alyssa said.

"Jack, help us out on this side," Triss said. "This is a better angle."

"All right." Jack prepared to jump across the hall. He

lined up a leap and dove for it, unaware that one of his boot lashings had come undone.

Jack tripped the moment he left cover. He found himself standing hunched over in the center of the hall, completely exposed.

A dozen laser shots zipped all around him. Miraculously, none connected.

Not wanting to chance it, he finished his run across the hall and ducked to safety with Triss and Finn.

"That was close!" he breathed.

"We need to press forward," Triss said. "Just seven more to take out and then we can run to the next intersection."

Jack dropped to his stomach and positioned himself below where Finn was standing and Triss was crouched.

The three of them took aim and fired at the five remaining guards in their line of sight, while Alyssa took out the two guards visible from her angle. The seven guards fell to the ground amid their slain comrades.

Jack rose to his feet. "Body count is kind of stacking up."

Alyssa assessed the pile of guards in the ineffective white armor. "That's what they get for trying to take us on."

"We're kind of terrible people, aren't we?" Jack realized.

The other three shrugged.

Jack brushed it off, and they resumed their forward push. Just shy of the intersection where the first wave of guards had taken up position, a new wave suddenly appeared down the hall. The guards began firing before Jack and the others could take cover.

A torrent of red blasts filled the corridor, completely surrounding the group. Yet, no one was struck.

"These guys have terrible aim," Finn laughed and continued walking forward, remaining unscathed by the enemy barrage.

Alyssa shook her head with disbelief. "I think they are literally not capable of hitting us."

Jack fired at one of the guards and his shot landed square in the guard's chest. "Meanwhile, I'm not even *trying* to aim and I hit them every time!"

"This is simultaneously awesome and ridiculous," Alyssa agreed as she also opened fire while continuing forward.

"Good to be us, I guess," Finn said as he took out another guard.

Triss laughed. "Look! I'm firing with my eyes closed and *still* have better aim than them!"

"I guess it won't be tough getting out of here after all," Alyssa said.

They continued working their way through the hall, firing randomly and taking out the guards while remaining untouchable. In short order, they reached the lobby where a final defensive line was waiting to stop them.

"You'll never get away!" one brave guard shouted. He released two dozen blasts at the group.

All the shots struck the floors and wall around them, forming a singed outline of where they were standing.

Alyssa smiled. "You get an 'A' for effort, but we'll be on our way now."

They walked out the door while the guards continued their hopeless assault.

"We'll get you!" one of the remaining guards called out. "You don't stand a—"

Jack blindly aimed behind him and took out the heckler. "Best heist ever."

CHAPTER 18

NOWHERE TO RUN

— — —

STILL laughing and joking while they casually strolled away from the GiganCorp lab, the group returned to the *Little Princess* with the MEC safely in hand.

"So, what's our next move?" Jack asked as soon as they were on the ship. He flopped down on the couch. "Getting the MEC was easy enough, but we still have the Vorlox after us, and your friends from Svetlana's crew need rescuing."

Alyssa frowned and took a seat at the galley table. "I just wanted to get the MEC and be done with everything. Why did the Vorlox have to come along and make everything complicated?"

Triss coughed into her hand, "Plot Device Principle."

Alyssa ignored her. "I guess we have no choice but to meet with the Vorlox and try to negotiate for our friends' releases."

"But where do we find the Vorlox?" Finn asked as he shoved Jack's legs aside to make room on the couch for himself to sit. "They told us to get the MEC in two days—

which we've now done—but there were no instructions about where to meet them."

"Maybe they'll find us?" Jack speculated.

"I don't want Svetlana or the others to get hurt." Alyssa shook her head. "I guess we just head up into space and see what happens."

Without further delay, Alyssa and Triss piloted the *Little Princess* into orbit.

"Should we stick around in this system?" Finn questioned when the main space station around the planet was visible out the window in the common area. "I mean, the guards had terrible aim so we got away, but what if GiganCorp sends the authorities after us?"

"Good point," Jack seconded. "We should probably put as much distance between us and this planet as we can."

"Sending the authorities after us would mean admitting what was stolen," Alyssa pointed out. "I'm not sure they're ready for the breakthrough to be public knowledge."

"There are ways to keep it vague enough," Triss countered. "We should play it safe."

"And what about the Vorlox? They probably know this is where we'd get the MEC, so it's a logical place for them to come looking for us," Alyssa stated. "If we go anywhere else, they might think we tried to run and will kill everyone."

"Maybe we should go back to the Winkelson station?" Triss suggested. "That's where we last encountered them and they told us to get the MEC for them."

"Yes, but I don't want to be implicated in the station's destruction or those deaths," Alyssa objected.

Jack raised his hand. "Not to be a downer, but we just killed about fifty people on camera."

Triss groaned. "You're right—we never set the camera on loop."

"Not to mention my mom," Alyssa realized.

"Outlaws!" Finn cheered.

"We have seen the power of reputation..." Triss mused.

"The possibility of warrants is a whole other matter and will have to wait," Alyssa said, refocusing. "We just can't get caught before we make sure our friends get free. Given that, we shouldn't go to the Winkelson station. The other place we've encountered the Vorlox is where *Luxuria* was destroyed."

"Where it all began," Jack murmured.

"How delightfully full-circle, I know." Alyssa took a resolute breath. "That's where we'll go."

The *Little Princess* made the jump to hyperspace moments later before anyone could think of another reason for them to do something different. In reality, there was no clear course of action. They had in their possession one of the greatest scientific breakthroughs in two centuries, authorities could come to arrest them at any moment, a band of potentially crazed killers was after them, and their friends' lives were on the line. Going anywhere was a risk, but at least going back to the site of a former home was a return to the familiar.

When the ship had completed its initial acceleration, Jack kicked Finn from the couch so he could stretch out. "I'm so tired. Hangover sleep is not good sleep."

"Well," Alyssa emerged from the cockpit, "this might be the perfect chance for me to test out the MEC's application with coffee brewing."

"Moment of truth!" Triss called out from her seat at the flight controls.

"If this doesn't work, then we can start working our way down the infinite list of other things we can do with it. But if it does..." Alyssa trailed off as she turned her attention to rummaging through the galley for the parts she needed to complete her contraption.

Jack watched her work on the galley table for the

next half hour, mounting components from other equipment to the frame of the existing coffee brewer. Based on the deftness of her movements, she must have theorized a design in the preceding months. Eventually, the MEC was the final piece to be bolted into place.

"This should do it..." Alyssa said at last. She loaded in the coffee beans and activated the machine.

A blue glow illuminated around the contraption and it hummed with the bright tone of an angelic chorus.

After ten seconds, the glow dissipated and the aroma of brewed coffee filled the cabin.

Alyssa removed the single-serve cup from the machine and waved it under her nose. "So far so good." She took a sip. "Stars! This—" She took another sip. "You have to try this!"

She ran to the cockpit and handed the cup to Triss. Her friend took the cup and smelled it cautiously. "It *does* have a great aroma." She took a sip. "WOW!"

The *Little Princess* rolled to the side as Triss' hand jerked on the controls.

"Let us in on it, come on!" Finn urged.

Alyssa returned to the common room and handed him the cup.

Finn sampled it. "Alyssa, you're a genius."

"My turn!" Jack pleaded. He took the cup from Finn, only to find that there was barely a sip left. He took the warm, brown liquid into his mouth. It was the perfect temperature to satisfy without risk of burning, and the flavor exploded on his taste buds. The coffee had none of the burned or bitter flavor he'd come to expect, but instead it was like his mouth had just been hugged by a chocolate teddy bear. "Wow... This coffee is, like, *really* good."

Alyssa's eyes lit up. "You really think so?"

"Absolutely. I could see this being the next big craze." Jack looked at the empty cup. "Can you make some more?'

Alyssa enthusiastically prepared second, and then third, portions for everyone. In case anyone wanted more later, she also filled a metal thermos with extra coffee, which would hold it at temperature for at least eight hours. Considering that they had no idea when, or if, the Vorlox would show up at their chosen destination, an energy boost might be needed later on.

The rest of the hyperspace jump was spent in a marvelous caffeine buzz. Jack made his bed and cleaned the bathroom, then completed all the dishes and straightened up the cabinets. Never had he felt so delightfully energized. The coffee must have had a similar effect on the others, as Jack noticed that Finn was organizing all the equipment for computer hacking and Triss appeared to be cleaning up the central database files while Alyssa programmed some new navigation subroutines.

By the time the *Little Princess* was preparing to drop out of hyperspace, the interior was ready for a photoshoot and the systems were operating with fifteen percent greater efficiency.

"I haven't been this productive and focused... ever!" Jack exclaimed. "I think you're really on to something with this MEC-brewed coffee, Alyssa."

"I was just going for flavor," she replied. "I never dreamed it'd have these bonus effects. It must have something to do with the energy field changing the chemical properties."

"Regardless of the science behind it, I'm hooked," Finn said.

"I never should have doubted you." Triss gave Alyssa a proud smile.

Alyssa beamed. "Thanks, guys."

The ship exited hyperspace a kilometer from the wreckage of the *Luxuria*. To their surprise, the Vorlox battleship was waiting for them at the broken structure.

"Well, looks like we guessed correctly," Jack said.

The front console beeped. "Incoming communication," Triss told them. She accepted the call.

The weapons on the Vorlox ship sprang to life—casings rolling back from the giant laser guns and massive hydraulic arms training the weapons toward the *Little Princess.* "Do you have the MEC?" the Vorlox representative asked over the comm.

"Are our friends okay?" Alyssa countered.

"They are fine," the Vorloxian replied. "And they won't be harmed so long as you give us the MEC without a fight."

The *Little Princess* lurched as it was suddenly grappled in a tractor beam and pulled toward the mammoth Vorlox ship. "Prepare to be boarded. You will hand over the MEC." The communication ended.

"I can try to break free..." Triss said.

"No, if we resist the others are as good as dead," Alyssa told her. "We'll need to pretend like we're cooperating until we can figure out another way for us all to escape."

"Um, would this be a bad time to point out that we can't fit everyone in here even if the Vorlox lets them go?" Jack asked.

"Yes," everyone replied in unison.

"In that case," Jack said, "I'll just say that it's great we got everything all cleaned up before we have company."

CHAPTER 19

TRAPPED

— — —

"WE can't just give the MEC to them until we know Svetlana and the others are safe." Alyssa ran from the cockpit into the common room to remove the MEC from the coffee maker. With the device in hand, she stood next to the galley, paralyzed with indecision. "Where can we hide it?"

"I don't know!" Jack looked frantically around the room. "One of the thermoses over there, maybe? Hurry!"

Alyssa dashed to the cabinet containing the drinkware and selected one of the polished metal thermoses. She unscrewed the top and dropped the MEC inside.

The *Little Princess* shuddered as it came to rest on the floor of the hangar within the Vorlox ship. Fists pounded on the outer door.

"What should I do with it now?" Alyssa hissed.

"Why are you asking me?" Jack shot back, glancing between her and the door. There was nowhere to go.

The door dropped open as the controls were

overridden from the outside.

The thermos launched from Alyssa's hands toward the galley counter. It landed on the countertop, knocking over the thermos filled with extra coffee. Both containers clattered onto the metal floor and one rolled under the couch.

"Hi! What can we do for you?" Jack greeted the Vorloxian soldier.

"Where is it?" the man demanded. He was wearing black body armor and his face was hidden behind a full helmet.

"Where's what?" Jack shrugged, trying to nudge the other thermos into hiding with his toe.

"The MEC. Hand it over now!" the Vorloxian demanded. "Is that it?" He spotted the thermos Jack was trying to hide and stepped toward it.

"Be careful with that!" Jack warned, trying to stall while he thought up a better plan. "It's... highly irradiated. It may cause a runaway reaction if it's opened in this small a space."

The soldier hesitated with confusion, and rightly so. "Radiation and air exposure aren't the same—"

"You don't have to take our word for it," Triss cut in. "But what would the other Vorlox say if you blew up the only working prototype of the MEC?"

"They would laugh," he replied.

Jack and Alyssa exchanged glances with Triss and Finn.

Jack decided to roll with it. "That's right—they would laugh. And just looking at you, I can tell that you are one to do the laughing, not the other way around."

"I crush anyone who laughs at me!" he bellowed.

"That's right! So let's not open that canister here, okay?" Alyssa suggested.

The soldier's gaze passed between them. "Fine. Come with me to Grant Pumba."

"You mean 'grand poobah'?" Triss clarified.

"What? No! Grant Pumba is the name of our mighty Vorlox leader."

Finn snickered. "Oh, this is all going swimmingly."

The guard carefully picked up the thermos from the floor and then ushered everyone off the ship.

Seven more Vorloxian soldiers were waiting in the hangar. They surrounded the crew of the *Little Princess* and directed them through a series of utilitarian hallways of polished steel and up a lift. Due to the elevator's small size, four guards first rode up with Jack and Alyssa, followed by the other four with Triss and Finn.

The destination floor had more refined finishes than the corridor leading from the hangar, including low-pile carpeting and integrated touch-displays in the walls.

"What is your leader going to do with us?" Alyssa asked the guards.

"He will need to tell you himself," one of the guards replied.

They reached the end of the hall, which terminated in a sliding door. The guards stepped forward and the door opened automatically, revealing a sophisticated conference room complete with an oblong conference table and holodisplay. Behind the table, a man and two women were seated in sleek swivel chairs.

The guards took up position along the front wall with four to either side of the entry door. The guard carrying the thermos stepped away from his post by the door just long enough to place the container in the center of the table within arm's reach of the three seated individuals.

"Please, take a seat," the man sitting in the chair at the center of the table said, gesturing to four chairs across from him. He was just past middle-aged and, like his female companions, appeared to be a completely normal human.

"Are you Grant Pumba?" Alyssa asked as she and the

others complied.

"I am," Grant confirmed, smoothing back his brown hair touched with gray. "I must apologize for all the armor and pistol secrecy. The MEC is very important, as you know."

"Don't take this the wrong way," Alyssa said hesitantly, "but you don't seem like the crazy murderers the rumors have made you out to be."

Grant laughed. "Oh, that all did get rather out of hand. It was necessary, though, to complete our work."

"What work is that?" Jack questioned.

Grant looked to the dark-haired woman on the left. She folded her hands on the tabletop. "My name is Irine," she stated. "I'm the Director of Research and Development for Competron."

Jack's mouth fell open. A quick glance to his right confirmed that his new friends were equally shocked.

Alyssa shook her head. "I'm confused."

"You're not the only mole to have ever been placed within a corporation, Alyssa," Irine stated. "Competron sent our own to GiganCorp, but unlike you with your position, ours came back to us. We learned that the MEC was almost production-ready and we needed to act."

"Most of the weapons and other dangerous black market tech circulating through the major channels originated with GiganCorp," Grant explained. "With the MEC on the verge of going public, we knew that anything that could be augmented with the MEC needed to be taken off the street while there was still an opportunity to do so."

"As the Director of Humanitarian Aid," the other woman at the table added, "it was clear to me that Competron would never be able to continue our mission-driven work if GiganCorp's products became little more than tools of destruction."

"And we couldn't go after GiganCorp directly," Grant continued, "so the next best thing was to take out the supply network for distributing those weapons. With that severed, even once the MEC was released, it would take much longer for the technology to work its way back into the hands of the truly dangerous individuals."

Irine nodded. "And to take out that network, we couldn't very well show up in Competron-branded ships. So, we invented the Vorlox persona as a distraction."

Grant examined the confused faces of the *Little Princess'* crew. "Everything you may have heard about us was part of that fabrication. In reality, our sole mission has been to take out the distribution network that could result in the MEC being used for harm."

"Is that why you blew up *Luxuria*?" Alyssa asked.

"That case is rather interesting," Grant replied, folding his hands on the tabletop. "It was the next target on our list, but when we arrived, the station had already been destroyed. We fired a warning shot at your ship when we spotted you, but you jumped to hyperspace."

"If you didn't destroy the station, then who did?" Alyssa asked.

"I don't know what to tell you," Grant said. "We picked up the escape pods from *Luxuria*—as we would anyway after taking out a base, to see if the weapon's dealers are open to an alternate career path. When we chatted with Svetlana, we learned that you, Alyssa, were a bridge between GiganCorp, Competron, and the mission of getting the MEC design out of GiganCorp's hands."

"Beth," Irine indicated the blonde woman to Grant's right, "had the idea to allow you to continue your mission to get the MEC with the hope you'd be successful and be open to siding with us once you knew what we were doing."

"How is Svetlana cooperating with you?" Alyssa asked. "She's was the top weapons dealer in this sector. I'd think she'd—"

"We offered her and the other members of her crew

jobs in medical sales. Very lucrative," Grant replied.

"Oh." Alyssa shrugged.

"And I do hope you'll consider working with us, as well," Beth said. "The MEC can help so many people if we leverage Competron's connections. You'd be well compensated."

It took Alyssa several seconds to find her voice. "What do you have in mind?"

"Improving planetary shields from stellar debris, power core for artificial organs to help the sick, portable electronics to bring education to children in remote settlements. The list goes on," Beth replied. "The heart of it, though, is we want to spread happiness."

"And all of that is possible with what you have hidden in this," Grant said, gazing with admiration at the thermos placed in the center of the table.

"They said it might explode," the guard who'd boarded the *Little Princess* warned from his post along the wall.

"I doubt that," Grant said, reaching for the thermos. He unscrewed the top. "Wait, what's this?" He stared with dismay at the contents and sniffed. "Is this coffee?"

"Ah, yeah, the MEC must be in the other thermos..." Jack mumbled.

Alyssa glared at him, then looked back to Grant. "I'm not convinced you're telling the truth. How can we know anything you said is true?"

Grant didn't seem to hear her. "Wow, this coffee smells incredible!" He took a small sip from the thermos. "Stars! This..." he took several gulps, "this is the most amazing coffee I've ever tasted! And I feel all tingly—and instantly energized! What's your secret?"

Alyssa's eyes widened with surprise. "Well, I was playing around with using the MEC as a power source..."

Grant grinned. "Forget everything I said before. This, right here, is the answer we've been looking for."

He passed the thermos to Beth and she tasted it.

"Stars, you're right! If anything would bring people together, it's this."

"Come again?" Finn asked.

"Making sure people are safe and smart is one thing, but a product like this would make them happy. No one would want to take up arms if they could start their day with a cup of this magical deliciousness," Grant said.

"You want to monetize it?" Alyssa asked.

"Oh yes," Grant confirmed.

"What happened to wanting to make sure they were telling the truth?" Jack asked her in a whisper.

"As long as we get paid, who cares?" she whispered back to him. Then, louder, "It's my design and I already had plans to bring it to market. If you want to use it, then you'll need to buy me out. And my friends here get a cut." She smiled at her companions.

"Do you have the actual MEC and the schematics?" Grant asked.

Alyssa nodded. "I do."

Grant smiled. "Then I think we can work out a deal."

CHAPTER 20

NEW HORIZONS

— — —

"I'VE NEVER BEEN rich before!" He still couldn't get over the number of decimal places now showing in his bank account balance—or the fact that the numeral was no longer red with a '-' in front of it. With his grandmother's expenses pre-paid for the next ten years, his warrants cleared and debts paid, the future possibilities were endless.

Alyssa seemed far less enthusiastic. "They're paying us to stay quiet about the Vorlox and Competron being one in the same. That kind of money isn't as satisfying as if we'd earned it."

"We'll get Spacecups up and running," Triss assured her. "I'm glad you didn't cave on those licensing rights."

"Yeah, I know." Alyssa sighed. "I guess part of me hoped I'd get away from corporate politics, but instead I'm locked in for life."

"Hey, money is money," Finn chimed in.

"I second that. We need to spend it!" Jack exclaimed.

Alyssa raised an eyebrow. "You're going to blow

through millions in a matter of days, aren't you?"

"Do you know how many gadgets I can get now? Plus, I can finally get my own ship like I always wanted," Jack replied. The *Little Princess* had been a compromise for his budget, but this was his chance to get a real ship with more than four compartments. With the seed money, he could even start a proper transportation business.

"You know," Finn ventured, "we could get an even *better* ship if we pooled our resources."

Alyssa and Triss exchanged glances. "I guess we did say we're a team now," Alyssa said. "I saw too many people drift apart because of money while I was growing up. I don't want the same to happen to us."

Triss nodded. "And, frankly, traveling through space alone is lonely and boring."

Jack lit up. "Does that mean we get to go spaceship shopping?"

Triss released a long breath. "I guess it does."

"Four cabins and a wet bar. That's all I ask," Finn stated.

"I like all of those things," Jack agreed.

"I'm sure we can agree on features we want," Alyssa said.

She was wrong.

The shopping expedition began well, with the team salivating over spacious floor plans and the latest interactive features. As they started to narrow down their options, however, it became clear that each person had a distinct vision of what features an ideal spaceship should contain.

"I don't know what you have against a round, rotating bed." Finn crossed his arms with a huff.

"I have nothing against the bed, just having it in the middle of the common room," Alyssa replied.

"The sparkling lights were a nice touch," Jack commented.

"We need something practical that will work for all of us," insisted Triss. She scanned over the digital catalogue again under the watchful eye of the shipyard proprietor. With the swipe of her hand, she selected a vessel they had previously bypassed due to its hefty price tag. "What about this one?"

A model of the gently used yacht appeared on the holoprojector. It was ten times the size of the *Little Princess* and at least three times as fancy, based on the interior images.

"Five cabins, three washrooms, separate galley, a *dining room*," Jack read off, excitement building in his chest.

Finn's eyes lit up. "Full-wall viewscreen across from a wet bar."

"And a bathtub!" Triss looked to Alyssa. "I want."

Alyssa evaluated the listing. "It's more than we budgeted."

"Hardly a constraining factor," Triss replied. "We've earned a little splurging. Plus, don't you want to be captain of something you can boast about?"

The shipyard proprietor waddled over to the sales kiosk, apparently having picked up on their interest. "She's a beaut, ain't see?" he said. "Got a few quirks, but what ship doesn't?"

"What's it called?" Alyssa asked.

"Registered name is the *Regency Star*, but you're welcome to change it when we transfer the ownership."

"That's a great name," Jack replied. It was regal, gender-neutral, space-y...

"I hate it," Alyssa stated.

Finn groaned. "Then we'll re-name it. Just look at that interior! We can spread out, and I could even fit a round bed in that starboard cabin."

Alyssa looked around at the faces of the crew. "Okay, fine. I'll agree to this ship, but on one condition."

—

Jack reclined on the palatial couch in the common room of the newly christened *Little Princess II.* "I could get used to this."

He'd hated Alyssa's name suggestion at first, but it somehow fit the vessel. The captain's condition to change the name had oddly unified the team, since they were first brought together by the original *Little Princess.* Jack never would have dreamed his short-lived ownership of the craft would have netted him friends and a major ship upgrade within a week, but he was happy to have fate finally smile upon him.

Not surprisingly, he'd been relegated to the worst sleeping chamber on the ship, which shared a wall with one of the washrooms. Though the washroom should have been for his sole use, and despite there being a preferable cabin amidships, the three other crewmembers had insisted that one of the washrooms and the other cabin be reserved for guests they would likely never have.

As a result, Jack was awoken every time Finn flushed the toilet in the middle of the night, or whenever the waste treatment system cycled—which was every half hour. The setup was less than ideal, but it was still a significant improvement over being subjected to Finn's night terrors.

The common area, at least, was an exquisitely appointed place for Jack to relax and feel like a full member of the crew. As Jack stretched out on his couch of choice, Finn reclined on an adjacent couch he'd adopted as his own, and Alyssa and Triss nestled into their plush, reclining chairs.

"We definitely made the right choice getting this ship," Alyssa said.

"We can really make it ours." Jack pondered various redecorating options that might elevate the neutral décor.

Finn rolled over so he could face the other members of the crew. "I almost don't know what to do with myself. It's been three whole days with no one trying to arrest us or shoot at us."

"No complaints here." Jack crossed his arms.

"It's great the Vorlox turned out to be friendly," Alyssa began, "but I can't help wondering who destroyed *Luxuria.*"

"Svetlana made a lot of enemies over the years. Whatever was going on with that, it's not our problem anymore," Triss replied.

Alyssa shook her head. "I'm not convinced she's going to let us go so easily."

"She did forgive Jack's debt," Finn pointed out. "Sounds like Competron offered her a good deal. Maybe she's turning over a new leaf."

"No, someone like her craves power. She'll get back in the game eventually," Alyssa said.

"Not our problem." Finn waved his hand.

Triss nodded. "Agreed. I'm choosing to focus on our good fortune. We have this beautiful new ship, and we can do anything we want."

"All right, I do have to admit that our newfound freedom is nice," Alyssa conceded. "Plus, that *galley*! I can really perfect the MEC-brewed espresso with that kind of workspace."

Jack smiled with contentment. He had no illusions that all dangers were behind them, but for the first time in years, he didn't have to worry about being destitute and homeless in the next day or week.

"I never thought I'd be on a ship like this," he murmured.

"Hey, you're *part owner* of this ship," Finn corrected.

"It's crazy. A week ago, I was scraping together every credit I could to pay for the *Lucile*—er, *Little Princess*. I know you begrudgingly let me stay, but seriously, it means a lot to be here with you."

Alyssa softened. "I think all of us have struggled to find a place to belong at one time in our lives or another. Having each other's backs is what separates us from some of the other criminal-types out there."

Finn nodded. "Except, we're supposed to be respectable businesspeople now."

"Technically, that wasn't part of the agreement with Competron," Triss countered. "They arranged for our outstanding warrants to be dismissed, but no part of that said we can't go back to our old ways."

Alyssa cast her a stern look. "We don't need the money. We've set out what we accomplished to do—break up the GiganCorp monopoly. Now we can travel and do whatever else we want. No need to get involved in anything shady."

Triss sighed. "I guess you're right. Maybe we can work our way through that travel guide of all the must-visit space station diners."

"Speaking of which," Finn said, "who's hungry for taquitos?"

THE END

ALSO BY A.K. DUBOFF

Troubled Space
Vol. 1: Brewing Trouble
Vol. 2: Stealing Trouble
Vol. 3: Making Trouble

Cadicle Space Opera Series
Book 1: Rumors of War (Vol. 1-3)
Book 2: Web of Truth (Vol. 4)
Book 3: Crossroads of Fate (Vol. 5)
Book 4: Path of Justice (Vol. 6)
Book 5: Scions of Change (Vol. 7)

Mindspace Series
Book 1: Infiltration
Book 2: Conspiracy
Book 3: Offensive
Book 4: Endgame

Dark Stars Trilogy
Book 1: Crystalline Space
Book 2: A Light in the Dark
Book 3: Masters of Fate

ABOUT THE AUTHOR

A.K. (Amy) DuBoff has always loved science fiction in all its forms, including books, movies, shows, and games. If it involves outer space, even better! As a full-time author, Amy primarily writes character-driven science fiction and science-fantasy with broad scope and cool tech. When she's not writing, she enjoys travel, wine tasting, binge-watching TV series, and playing epic strategy board games.

www.akduboff.com

Printed in Great Britain
by Amazon

40151152R00078